Roy and Rosie,

It was great seeing you both again! Thanks for bringing Ty and Anika, it made a great vacation better!

I hope you enjoy my story...

Rick

The Man
in the
Cinder Clouds

Rick Daley

The Man in the Cinder Clouds

ISBN: 1461091683
ISBN-13: 978-1461091684

Interior book design by Rick Daley
Cover design by CreateSpace

To everyone who has ever taken a leap of faith:
May you land where you intended.

And, of course, to my family, for putting up with me
and supporting me in (almost) everything I do.

CONTENTS

CHAPTER 1

AN ICE SURPRISE

Jason thought going to the North Pole with his dad would be cool, but it wasn't. It wasn't cool at all. Well, aside from the temperature—that was freezing.

Back at home, Jason's dad joked around and played games with him. They did everything together. But at the North Pole, Jason learned adults are a lot different at work. His life was made up of not touching things, not bothering people, and not getting in the way.

Jason pushed back the hood of his parka and sat down at his father's desk.

Alone.

Again.

Everyone else was next door, in the lab building. *The Forbidden Zone.* The one place in the entire North Pole where interesting things happened was the one place Jason could not go.

Jason reached to the floor and picked up a long, triangular block of wood. His father's name was engraved on one side. His fingers traced the letters in the wood: *Professor Hodgin.* He wanted to set it on the desk so the name faced the door, but there wasn't any room among the piles of folders and books. He set the block back on the floor. Everyone there knew his dad, anyway.

Four weeks at the North Pole. Two down and two to go. His dad said it would be "a bonding experience" that would help Jason "build character." His mom said it was "a plan that looked better on paper." Turned out Mom was right. As usual.

In the beginning it was awesome. They took a huge ship deep into the Arctic Ocean. Jason stood at the bow of the ship with his dad and watched the strong steel hull cut through the ice until the ship couldn't go any farther. Then he got to ride in a helicopter called Blackbird. The pilot, Dan, landed Blackbird right on the ship's deck to pick them up. Dan flew Jason and his dad to the research camp at the North Pole.

The mission: To drill for ice cores. The work was important—something to do with global warming—but Jason wasn't too interested in the details.

He just wanted to see Santa Claus.

Last year at Christmas Jason's big brother Justin told him Santa wasn't real, but Jason didn't believe him. Why should he? Justin lied about Tabasco sauce being sweet. And he was totally wrong about fire ants.

Jason wanted nothing more than to prove to Justin that Santa Claus was real. He brought a camera—vowing to never set it down—confident he would be the first to get photo evidence of an elf, a flying reindeer...or maybe even the Big Man himself, out on a stroll with Mrs. Claus.

The North Pole lost its luster before Blackbird even landed. Christmas Village didn't appear in the snow. There were no toy factories, no fields of reindeer games...not even a single Christmas tree. Just a few stuffy scientists and a whole lot of cold.

In the first few days, Jason asked several of the research assistants about Santa. Most of them had been to the North Pole several times before. They all chuckled and winked at each other when they told Jason they may have glimpsed Santa once, or they thought they saw reindeer tracks in the snow. Day after day, Jason stared through the foggy windows at the frozen wasteland that surrounded him as far as the eye could see. As he did he slowly convinced himself that Santa Claus was not real.

Of all the things for Justin to finally be right about, it had to be this.

His dad tried to play it off and said they weren't right on top of the North Pole, just near it. He told Jason there were really two North Poles: One was the Geographic North Pole and the other was the North Magnetic Pole, and nobody knew which one Santa picked. It didn't matter to Jason. He was convinced Santa couldn't live up there anyway.

Nobody could.

The North Pole was a bleak environment, an enormous expanse of snow-topped ice floating upon the Arctic Ocean. Sometimes Jason could feel the ice moving underneath him. The cracks and pops echoing through its vast white stretches made him feel that any second the ice could open up and swallow him down to the frigid depths of the water below.

He looked out the window at the sun as it traced its slow circle around the horizon. All day and all night, the sun was there. It rose a little higher in the sky each day. His dad said the sun would not set until September, which was still five months away.

Jason's stomach rumbled. He looked across the crowded room at the clock on the wall. Both hands pointed to twelve, but he wasn't sure if it was noon or midnight.

He reached into his coat pocket and pulled out an apple. His dad insisted he eat one each day, since they didn't have a doctor at the North Pole. He couldn't bite directly into the apple because of his braces. He looked around for the slicer but he couldn't see it for all the clutter. Every flat surface in the room was covered with books, magazines, and manila folders stuffed to the gills with papers and held closed with thick rubber bands. The only clear surface was the bottom of the garbage can—which was spotless, still awaiting its first piece of trash.

The hinges on the door squeaked. Jason looked up as his father walked into the small office and went straight to a pile of books on the floor next to the desk. His dad pulled a book from the middle of the stack, extracted a note that was stuck to one of the pages, set the book back down, and turned to leave.

"Dad?" Jason asked.

His dad walked out and the door swung closed.

Jason stared at his apple. *Heck with the stupid braces, anyway.* He opened his mouth to take a bite when his dad poked his head back into the office.

"Did you need something?"

Jason held up the apple. "Do you know where the slicer is?"

His dad lifted a stack of folders teetering at the corner of the desk. The apple slicer was underneath it. His dad set the stack of folders on a pile of magazines. "Here," he said, holding his hand out.

Jason handed him the apple. His dad held the slicer flat and pressed down on top of the apple. He pulled the stem and a round apple core rose from the center of the fresh cut slices. The trash can welcomed its first entry with a dull thud.

"Nice core. Can I take it to the lab and study it?" Jason said.

"No time for games. We found an unusually deep patch of ice. We can't even detect the bottom of it. Blackbird radioed in and said a forty-foot core is on its way. It's the deepest sample ever taken from the Arctic, and I'll be the first to read it!"

"You're almost as excited as Mom was when she was reading those vampire books."

"Different kind of reading, Jason. This is a different kind of reading entirely—"

A young intern burst into the room. "Professor Hodgin, come quick!" She tried to catch her breath. "You won't believe this!"

"What is it, Rebecca?"

"The ice core is here, and there's something stuck in it. It looks like a stack of papers, or a book or something," she said.

"Probably trash from some former research team."

"Professor, it's over ten meters down."

"That's impossible! It would have to be nearly a thousand years old...That would pre-date the first Arctic explorers by—"

"I need to get you to the lab so you can see for yourself."

Professor Hodgin looked at his son. "I stand corrected," he said. "Maybe it is the same kind of reading."

Rebecca tugged on the sleeve of Professor Hodgin's parka. "Let's go," she urged and they raced from the room.

Jason grabbed a slice of apple and stuck it in his mouth. As he started to chew his dad poked his head back in the room. "Are you coming, or what?" he asked.

Jason nearly choked on his apple.

CHAPTER 2
NO ORDINARY BOOK

Jason zipped his coat and bundled up against the Arctic winds. He followed his father and Rebecca across the ice to the lab building—a long, narrow half-cylinder that looked like a Pringles can that fell over and sank into the snow, except it wasn't red. It was the ugliest color of gray imaginable.

Once inside the lab building they had to stop in a small room and put on special suits before entering the lab itself. They kept their parkas on under the baggy suits; the lab was extra cold so the ice cores would not melt. They even had to wear special masks called respirators so their breath wouldn't contaminate the core samples.

The research team was gathered along one side of a long table that ran down the center of the lab. Fans hummed along the other side of the table, blowing cold air across the forty-foot cylinder of ice.

The top of the ice core was white with fresh snow and grainy like sand. A couple feet down it became dense and opaque as each year's new snow weighed down on its predecessors. Ten feet down the ice was clear, and as Jason looked farther down the core he noticed that it started to turn blue.

The core had lines running up and down like the bar codes he helped scan on the U-Scan at the grocery store. The lines marked off years like tree rings until they hit a dark, dense band—the cover of an ancient book—about thirty feet from the top of the core. A dingy yellow section followed—pages—and then another thick dark band comprised the back cover and the book yielded again to the ice; a lonely relic left frozen in time centuries ago by...whom?

"This is incredible," Professor Hodgin whispered. He gently grabbed hold of the ice core on each side of the book and pulled. The book came loose with a pop, like it was vacuum-sealed. It spun like a top, fell over, and wobbled to a halt. It looked like a Halloween Oreo, the kind with the orange double-stuffing.

"We just punched through the center of the book. It looks like a clean cut. We need to go get the rest of it," Professor Hodgin said.

No one moved.

"Come on people, let's go while it's still daytime!"

"Dad, it'll be daytime until September," Jason said.

"Well...the ice may melt before then. We better dig before this turns into a fishing expedition!"

People scattered left and right to prepare. They packed picks and shovels onto skids, which were then hitched to snowmobiles. They loaded heavy drilling equipment into Blackbird. Jason and his father climbed into the helicopter.

"You buckled?" Dan asked.

Jason and his father gave Dan a thumbs-up.

"Hold on, then."

The engines roared and Blackbird took flight. They flew low and fast. Jason looked down at the ice and snow zipping away beneath him. When they circled to land Jason peered into a huge crevice near the drill site. He couldn't see the bottom of the deep blue canyon.

Jason tapped his father on the shoulder and pointed out the window. "What *is* that?" he asked over the roar of the engines.

"We don't know. It shouldn't be here. The ice should only be three to five meters deep, but it's well over a hundred. That's why we picked this spot to drill."

Dan set Blackbird down on the ice. When the snowmobiles got there they started digging. They chipped away at the ice for two days. They dug the hole wide in case there were other books, but there were not. Just one book, frozen deep in a block of ice...a block that was bigger and deeper than any other ice in the Arctic Ocean. With the greatest care they lifted the book from its frozen repository and prepared it for the journey back to the lab.

What they had to do next was harder than digging through forty feet of solid ice: They had to separate every page and match up the round section from the ice core with the rest of the book.

Three days later they were finally ready to crack the cover.

The book sat on a large table in the lab. The cover was a beautifully polished piece of wood, free of words or markings of any kind (except for the round scar from the drill that dug the ice core). Professor Hodgin sat on a chair at the head of the table. Jason stood next to him, and the rest of the research team gathered round. His father lifted the cover.

Jason read the first page out loud: "The Man in the Cinder Clouds."

"Wait, you can read Spanish?" asked Juan Gonzalez, a research assistant from Puerto Rico.

"What?" Jason asked.

"That's written in Spanish," Juan pointed to the words. "*El hombre en las nubes de ceniza.*"

"What about these Japanese characters?" asked Professor Nara, pointing at the page. "But I don't see Spanish letters."

"I can only read English," Jason said. "I don't see *any* other letters or words."

"It looks like whoever is reading the book can automatically see it in their native language," Professor Hodgin said. "Incredible!"

Professor Hodgin turned to the next page, which was dense with writing. The script seemed to jump and dance, excited that someone had finally come along to read the tale it told. Letters looped into words, and flags waved from each sentence, flying mid-staff on some letters and dangling from the tips of others. And just like the title page the words spoke to all readers in their native tongue.

The top-right corner of the page had a picture of a wooded area, with many trees and small animals, and little pointy-eared elves. Everybody looked busy, except in the center there was a young man with red hair and a bushy red beard sleeping under the branches of a large evergreen tree.

Everyone took a seat around the table as Professor Hodgin started reading. "Once upon a time..."

CHAPTER 3
LITTLE BOY LOST

Once upon a time, deep in the forest near the Great Glen of the Woodland Elfs, a female Elf named Kristina Kringle went out on a stroll with her infant son, Eldwin. Just outside the boundaries of the Glen she found a human baby swaddled in torn rags, lying in the brush and abandoned to die. Being an Elf and a lover of all things living she took the baby boy home with her and nursed him back to health.

Our Elfin laws of old minced no words in forbidding contact with humans. When the High Council found out about the baby they demanded that Kristina return the boy to his human family immediately.

She refused.

Kristina argued that he had been left to die and had no family to take him in. She pleaded with the High Council to let her keep the baby, reasoning that her milk gave the infant its new life, and it was thus part Elf.

After much deliberation, the High Council finally agreed to let Kristina and her husband raise the boy alongside their own son.

She named the baby Kris, after herself. Kris Kringle.

It is about this special man-Elf, Kris Kringle, that I have the fortune to tell you...

* * *

Kristina's Elfin milk affected her adopted son in many ways. It gave him the strength and speed of an Elf, and it enabled him to communicate with plants and animals as we do. And while he does not share our immortality, it is said that his lifespan will be measured in millennia.

But despite all the Elfin qualities he had taken on, there were still many human traits that set Kris apart from the rest of us. Take, for example, his hair: Kris Kringle's head was topped with curly red hair, and a bushy red beard graced his cheeks. Then, as now, we Elfs sport only black or blonde hair that does not curl, nor does hair grow upon Elfin faces. And although Kris didn't grow tall by human standards, for a Woodland Elf he was gargantuan (a full head taller than the tallest Woodland Elf, so I am told).

Kris grew up to be a fine young man-Elf, respectful but fun-loving, and although the majority of Elfs had no issue with him he often had special encounters with the High Council. You see, there was one particular human trait he retained that we Elfs do not share: The need for sleep...a need that was often in conflict with the need to work. (Indeed, many Elfs still argue that sleep is an affliction no amount of Elfin milk could ever cure.)

The most outstanding difference in Kris, however, is his thought-hearing. While we Elfs can hear the thoughts of other Elfs near us as if they were spoken aloud, we cannot hear Kris Kringle's thoughts; nor can Kris Kringle hear the thoughts of any Elf.

Kris Kringle can hear the thoughts of humans.

So strong is his connection to the humans that when Kris closes his eyes and concentrates he can see detailed visions projected from the hearts and minds of people all over the world.

In his youth, Kris watched those visions night and day. He was trying to find his human family. He looked the world over, hoping for a clue to help him discover who he really was. And eventually he did find someone that changed him—and us—forever. It started in the first moon of the fall, in the year 51,413 on the Elfin Calendar...

CHAPTER 4

A RUDE AWAKENING

Kris Kringle slept under the drooping branches of a large fir tree. He smiled through his bushy red beard and let out an occasional laugh, "Ho-ho-ho." (Always a ho-ho-ho, his laugh. Never a ha-ha or a hee-hee. Always a ho, and always three at a time. A most peculiar trait.)

Kris' brother Eldwin happened by, looking for Kris. Eldwin was the most gifted carpenter in the Glen. Then, as now, the primary duty of Woodland Elfs was to keep trees alive and healthy, so carpentry was practiced with a high degree of reverence. Eldwin's skills were admired by all Woodland Elfs, for he gave fallen trees a second life as a house, a chair, a wagon, a toy...His apprentice Kris, however, was a different story. Try as he might, Kris' best efforts at carpentry generally resulted in a lot of sawdust and little else. Alas, he was destined for other things.

But carpentry was not why Eldwin was out looking for Kris. Eldwin—the Highest Ward of the Firs—was looking for Kris—the Second Highest Ward of the Firs—because Kris was three groves behind in his duties.

Eldwin nudged Kris, trying to wake him, but it didn't work. Eldwin turned and saw Haelan, head of the High Council, and gave Kris a swift kick in the rump, desperate to rouse his brother from his slumber before Haelan spotted him. Kris stirred, then slumped down farther and began to snore.

Haelan's pointed ears wiggled and he turned toward the noise. Seeing Kris sleeping under the branches of the fir tree, Haelan shook his head. Eldwin began to stammer out an excuse for Kris, but Haelan held up a hand to silence him.

"If all Elfs were to sleep instead of respecting their duties the forest would wither and the land would go barren and lifeless. Do you agree, Kris Kringle?" Haelan asked.

Kris opened his eyes at the sound of Haelan's voice and stood up quickly. It would have been wise of him to stand up slowly. Then he might have noticed the branch above his head. A loud *thonk* made him well aware of the tree's limb—just a bit too late—and he sat back down fast, rubbing his head.

"I do agree, yes. But if I may explain..." Kris started.

"You may explain, but not here and not to me alone. You shall explain to the High Council at noon today."

"Yes sir, of course."

"And Kringle..."

"Yes?"

"Make sure you are not late again." Haelan walked off into the woods.

Kris crawled out from under the tree and stood up, stretching his arms wide as he let out a big yawn.

"What time is it?"

"It's ten o'clock. You must learn to stay awake, Kris. This is the third time this month you've been summoned to the High Council. There's talk they may banish you," Eldwin warned.

"This is the first I've slept in three moons, and I've had only an hour of rest. I fight it as long as I can, but I can't stay awake forever. It's the human in me. They sleep every night, you know."

"Yes, I know. But the Council sees it as a dangerous connection to the human world. That and your search for your family. They are afraid you are going to lead humans here."

Kris nodded and sighed. "I can't stop, though. I'm getting close to finding my family. I can feel it. But the Council needn't worry. The humans can't see me like I can see them. It's a shame the Council can't see the beauty in humanity as I can."

"It's not that humanity is without beauty. It's without virtue. All humans are greedy and destructive at heart."

"That's not true!"

"According to the High Council it is. I don't know why you keep trying to prove them wrong. Assuming human virtue actually *does* exist, Haelan wouldn't notice it if it was impaled on his ears. All any Council member sees is the path of human destruction—fallen trees and slain animals. And starving babies left to die in the wood."

Kris nodded. In his visions he saw the naughty as well as the nice. "Perhaps today will be the day that I convince the Council otherwise."

"Good luck with that one," Eldwin said and patted his brother on the back and strode off into the woods.

Kris went about his chores, checking trees for boring bugs and moldy needles.

* * *

Kris finished inspecting his second grove of pines and decided to get a drink. He spotted Elaana sitting by the stream's edge. A baby bunny nibbled a flower that lay on her palm.

Elaana's face was the definition of Elfin beauty. Her nose, tiny like a flower bud, offset her two blue almond-shaped eyes. Her cheekbones rose high above her softly pointed chin and ever-smiling lips. And her face was framed by silky black hair that never seemed to be tangled or out of place, even when flying in the strongest wind.

Elaana stirred the hearts of many young male Elfs, but was never approached for marriage—as Haelan's daughter, none were brave enough to ask her father for her hand.

Kris waved to her. She didn't look up. "Hey Elaana!" Kris called. The noise startled the bunny. It scuttled and slipped off the bank and into the swift water. Kris sprinted and plunged into the water, snatching the baby bunny from the current before its head went under.

"I'm sorry, I didn't mean to scare her," Kris said, handing the bunny to Elaana.

Elaana blushed but didn't say anything.

"I just came to get a drink, but I can come back later," Kris said.

"No, stay and drink, please. Sorry. I forget that you can't hear my thoughts," Elaana said. The rose petals left her cheeks and they returned to their milky white.

Elaana dried the bunny off and set it on the ground. It hopped away to find its mother. Kris squatted and dipped his hand in the water. He drank with a loud slurp and stood up. Droplets rolled down his beard and a small belch escaped before he could stop it. Elaana giggled and Kris covered his mouth with his hand.

"Excuse me. That happens when I get tired."

"Sneak off and sleep, then. I'll cover for you. What chores do you have?"

"I still have one more fir grove to tend to. Then I have to meet the High Council at noon."

"Again?"

"Yep." Kris looked up at the sun. It was getting close to its mid-day peak. "I'm afraid it's too late for you to help me with your father this time." He stretched and yawned. "I need to get going."

"I'll look after the fir grove for you. Catch a quick nap. You'll need your wits about you when you meet with the Council."

"You don't have to—"

"Go, rest. Don't worry. I've been with birds and bunnies all morning. I could really stand for the peaceful company of trees right now. They don't stumble into streams when friends come by."

"Thank you," Kris said, and headed off into the woods.

"Anytime."

CHAPTER 5

A FAMILY IS FOUND

Eldwin searched throughout the Glen for Kris. He found him in a grove of pines, nestled in a soft bed of needles, eyes closed.

"Wake up! It's five after twelve. You're late for your meeting. How can you sleep at a time like this?"

"I'm not asleep. I'm watching." Kris opened his eyes.

Eldwin hid his face in his hands. "Oh, no. That's worse! This will not bode well. I'm afraid of what they're going to do to you. This is going to break Mom's heart. You know how hard she fought to keep you. Losing you would kill her. And she's immortal, so that's pretty bad, you know."

Kris stood up and brushed the pine needles off his clothes. He put his hands on Eldwin's shoulders and looked his brother in the eye. "I know where they are."

"Who?"

"My family! Well, distant relatives at least. I've tracked them down to a place called Oldenton. I'm going to ask the Council to let me make contact."

"Are you kidding? This is going to get you banished for sure!"

"Don't worry. It's all part of my master plan."

"You actually have a plan...What are the chances of that?"

"What do you think?" Kris said and winked.

Kris and Eldwin walked to the center of the Glen. They stopped at the wide base of an ancient tree, the tallest in the forest. A door opened in its trunk, revealing a hollow center. Kris entered and turned back to face his brother.

"They'll never agree to it, you know," Eldwin said. Kris laid his finger aside his nose and he smiled and winked at Eldwin before rising up the shaft to the top of the tree.

Kris stepped out onto a large, round platform and found thirteen very disapproving glares waiting for him. He took a deep breath and then smiled and stepped forward.

"You're late. Again." Haelan's glare was particularly disapproving. "I suppose you have an excellent reason for your tardiness. Please share it with us."

"I was watching the humans."

A hush fell over the platform. Birds and insects stopped their calls as the High Council silently debated.

Haelan spoke for the Council. "This is not the first time we Elfs have been delayed in our duties on account of your fascination with the humans. We are the caregivers of the trees. When our jobs go undone it impacts the health of the entire Glen as it does the forests beyond."

"I know. I think we can make this work, though," Kris said. "I have a plan."

Haelan looked at the other members of the High Council. They nodded in agreement. "Continue."

"I know there has been talk of banishing me. I don't want to leave the Glen forever. But I was born human, that we can't deny. I sleep."

"Kris, it's not just the sleeping. It's your...urges. You can't keep your mind off the humans, and we are afraid you will lead them here."

"I know. I hear their deepest wishes. I try to block it out, but I can't. I don't know why this gift is so strong, but it is, and I know I am meant to use it."

"To what end? To find your family? It's nonsense. Kris, you're 122 years old. Any family you had must have died years ago. We've been over this a thousand times. Humans don't live as long as we do."

"No, but they do have more babies. I found distant relatives in a place called Oldenton. It's far away, across the water. I want to go there. I want to make contact."

"Absolutely not!" The Council members spoke in unison. "Kris, if you make contact with a human—family or not— you will immediately be banished for life, and not just from our Glen. No Elfin community will have you, anywhere. That rule has been in place for eons and we will not be the Elfs to see it broken," Haelan warned.

"But why was the rule made? Humans are not all bad. They do have virtue."

"Humans are bringers of war and takers of life. Any virtue they show is a ruse."

"But is the fox any less clever when it raids the chicken coop? Or the wolves when they encircle a wounded fawn? Those animals are takers of life, yet they are welcome in every Elfin Glen."

Haelan gasped. "Are you proposing we bring the humans here?"

"No! Let me explain, please. The humans are just like the other animals—"

"Other animals do not tear down the trees for buildings and reshape the land for their own purpose. That's a human trait."

"Is human construction that much different from a bird's nest? Even Elfs build with wood."

Haelan shook his head. "We use fallen limbs. A human would destroy an entire tree only to use one small branch."

"Beavers cause destruction to the living trees and change the land, as does any animal that digs a burrow, from the field mouse to the bear. But we offer these animals our protection and understanding. Why the grudge against the humans? They're just bigger animals, and there are more of them. They can't help that they have a bigger impact on the world around them."

"Kris, the animals you mentioned do not pose us a direct threat. Humans do. They will destroy our land—not for the building of their homes, but for the simple fact that it is there. Evil resides in the human heart. They enslave animals. They even enslave other humans. You can't live among them. You are different. They will not accept you for who you are."

"And who am I? I don't fit in here just like I won't fit in there. I'm as much human as I am Elf. More, actually. Am I not proof that humans can have virtue?"

"That's due to your Elfin upbringing, not your humanity. No humans are born with virtue. Go, use your powers and look the world over. Look for a human born with true virtue. If you can actually find one, we will consider your proposal."

Kris smiled. "I already know of one."

Haelan raised his eyebrows and cocked his head.

"Who?"

"Jesus."

* * *

Kris slept while the High Council debated. For hours the silent conversation ensued. When Kris woke the next morning, it was agreed: They would consider his proposal.

Kris told them his master plan. The High Council debated the merits of the plan, and its risks. They kept talking all through the next day and into the wee hours of the morning beyond. Notes were taken as the plan was modified. Eventually they all stopped talking and writing.

Haelan sat back in his chair. The nighttime insects sang in the trees around them and the moon shone high in the sky above. "So are we in agreement?"

"We are," Kris said as he finished his third read-through of a long scroll. Kris signed the scroll, as did every member of the High Council.

"I wish you luck, Kris Kringle," Haelan said as he handed Kris the scroll. "Although I believe you are grossly underestimating how difficult your journey will be. I fear we will never see you again. Remember, you are not measured by the challenges you face in life, but rather by the steps you take to overcome them."

"I'll be back before the earth runs a full course around the sun. I promise," Kris said. "And I'm a man of my word."

CHAPTER 6

THE RULES

Kris and Eldwin sat atop a hill overlooking the river. "I told them my master plan," Kris said. "We discussed it for many hours."

"Are they going to let you go through with it?"

"Yes."

Eldwin stood up. "Really?"

"No."

"I thought so."

"At least not the way I originally wanted to. We had to modify the plan a little bit."

Eldwin's pointed ears perked up. "How much?"

"A little bit."

Kris pulled out the scroll and let one end drop. The scroll rolled down the long hill until it hit the trunk of a tree one-hundred feet away. The scroll bounced to the left, and then continued down the hill for another thirty feet before coming to rest against a big rock. Eldwin looked at the procession of words marching down the hill in small Elfin print, like a thousand armies of ants on their way to fill the remainder of a scroll that was only half unraveled.

"I'd hate to see your version of a lot," Eldwin muttered.

The title at the top of the scroll read:

RULES AND BYLAWS
GOVERNING THE ESTABLISHMENT
OF THE INAUGURAL CHRISTMAS
DURING WHICH KRIS KRINGLE
WILL ENGAGE IN
LIMITED HUMAN CONTACT

Eldwin let out a low whistle. "Limited Human Contact. What are the limits? Did they let you keep any of your ideas?"

"Oh, yes. My plan is in here..." Kris scanned the visible portion of the scroll. "Somewhere. We cut a few things out. Haelan added a couple stipulations of his own—"

Eldwin laughed and pointed at the scroll. "A couple?"

"It's not that bad, really," Kris assured him.

"How did you pull this off?"

"I told them I tracked my family down to Oldenton and I asked to make contact. The Council said no."

"You don't need thought-hearing to see that one coming."

"But I told them Elfin law requires me to make contact."

"How hard did you hit your head on that tree? No Elfin law requires human contact!"

"But Elfin law does require a gathering to celebrate when a child is born into a family. That's not just a tradition, they wrote that down. It doesn't matter if it's a distant Glen, either. A gathering is required. Since I'm 122 years old, I'm way overdue."

"Yeah, but you're talking about humans here. And Oldenton is not a Glen."

"And I am not an Elf. I have a human family. The actual word of law is 'Glens and other habitats' so Oldenton is covered."

"So what do you do, knock on the door and say, 'Hi, I'm your long-lost half-Elf cousin?'"

"Not quite. I'm not really sure which door to knock on."

"What do you mean?"

"I know they live in Oldenton, but I'm not sure which family it is."

"So what do you do, walk into the center of town and yell, 'Who wants to meet their long-lost half-Elf cousin?'"

"I wish! I must stay hidden from view. But I'm allowed to leave an anonymous gift for every child in Oldenton."

Eldwin laughed. Kris didn't.

"You're serious?"

Kris nodded.

"Well dip me in Faerie dew. Why no adults?"

"Haelan said human children are 'considerably less wicked' than adult humans. I didn't argue that point. We just picked a day, and that was that..."

Eldwin took the scroll from Kris. "Rule 1: *Kris Kringle must leave the Glen immediately and never come back.* I don't believe it! You agreed to this?"

"I did, but—"

"How could you? Did you think about our parents? Did you think about me? Or Elaana?"

"What has Elaana got to do with this?" Kris asked.

"She really likes you."

"She does?"

"You can't tell? You may be able to read the minds of humans but you're blind to Elfs, that's for sure!"

Kris' face glowed as red as his hair. "I still get to come back."

"But right here it says never! N-E-V-E-R."

"There's a loophole. Rule 3,095, subsection B, topic 19–F: *Should Kris Kringle bring back proof that Human Virtue exists in the world today, he may return to the Glen.*"

Eldwin slapped his palm to his forehead. "Good luck with that one! Prove human virtue? Kris, you make it sound half-reasonable when you *suggest* it exists, but how on earth can you actually bring back proof?"

Kris shrugged. "I don't know how yet. I just know that I will."

Eldwin scoffed. "I knew you didn't have a plan. Why did you let them talk you into leaving?"

"That was my idea, actually. It's for the safety of the Glen and all the Elfs. If I get caught, I can't lead any humans back here. I have to set up a base camp somewhere remote, where humans can't go."

Eldwin read further down the scroll. "What makes December 25 so special?"

"For the humans December 25 is Christmas Day, and many of them celebrate the birth of a man named Jesus. If ever there was a human born with virtue, it was Jesus. Even the High Council agreed to that."

"Why? What did Jesus do?" Eldwin asked. Like most Elfs of the time, he was completely ignorant regarding human history and culture.

"He taught people 'do unto others as you would have them do unto you.' He gave selflessly to others, helping the needy and healing the sick. His actions fit directly with Elfin philosophy. Plus there is a tradition of gift-giving at Christmas. Rule Number 53: *Kris Kringle may leave behind a gift for each child in Oldenton.*

"And look here," Kris pointed at the scroll. "I did this for you. Rule 53-A: *Any child who wishes to receive a gift must leave out an evergreen branch by the fireplace on Christmas Eve.* I know how fond you are of conifers." Kris patted Eldwin on the arm.

"Thanks, I guess," Eldwin said. He read down the scroll. "Rule 367: *Kris Kringle can only bring the children the gift they wish for.* How will you know what they wish for?"

"I can read their minds, remember?"

"Yes, but how will they know to even make the wish?"
Kris stroked his beard. "You know, we never thought of that. I'll have to ask."

"You can't! If you bring this up to the High Council they may change their minds about the whole operation."

"I'm not going to ask the High Council. I'm going to ask the children of Oldenton."

"Oh. How will you do that without being seen?"

"I can talk to them. The rules say I can't be seen, but it doesn't say anything about them hearing me. I'll come at night. That's the other reason I picked Christmas, anyway. It's right after the Winter Solstice, which is the shortest day of the year and therefore the longest night. It buys me extra time under cover of darkness."

"But still, deliver a gift to every child in Oldenton in one night? That's a lot of work for one person." Eldwin kept reading the scroll.

"It doesn't have to be that way. Rule 781: *Any Elf who wants to accompany and assist Kris Kringle may do so.*"

Eldwin read down the scroll until he found Rule 781. But then he read Rule 782 aloud: "*Any Elf who chooses to assist Kris Kringle must leave the Glen, never to return.*"

"Don't worry about that. The loophole covers us all. Once I prove human virtue, we'll be welcome back. Will you come with me?"

"What can I do?" Eldwin asked.

"Human children love toys made of wood, and you're the best carpenter in the Glen. You can be in charge of the toy factory."

"That sounds interesting..."

"Well, first you'll have to *build* a toy factory, but then you'll be in charge of it. But you'll have other Elfs to help you. If all goes according to plan. Oh, but you'll also have to build their homes. I guess there's a lot of building with this job..."

"Where do you plan on doing this, anyway?"

"At the Great Northern Glen."

"What? You *are* crazy. Kris, the Great Northern Glen is a Faerie tale! Trust me, I know several Faeries, and they would agree."

"The legend began with the Elfs, not with the Faeries. Elfs are creatures of truth. I believe the Great Northern Glen exists."

"There's nothing up there except snow and ice. There are no trees, no Glen..."

"In which case, it's an even better idea. The humans will never find us there," Kris said. "We also have as much room as we want, we can spread out and work in comfort."

"And cold," Eldwin added.

"We get plenty of snow in the Glen. Really, how bad can it be?"

"I guess we'll find out," Eldwin said. "What else does this scroll say that I need to know about?"

Kris took the scroll and scanned it. "You should probably know about Rule 1,845. And Rule 2,157. And Rule—"

"How about I just read it for myself?"

"Good luck with that one," Kris said, and handed Eldwin the scroll.

CHAPTER 7
LEAVING THE GLEN

Kris left Eldwin alone to read the scroll and headed home to pack. When he arrived he found his mother waiting for him in the kitchen.

"Word spreads fast in the Glen, you know." Kristina tapped her temple. "Are you sure this is what you want?"

"I have to do it. I don't have a choice."

"You always have a choice. Remember that. Life presents us with many paths. Which one you take is up to you."

They sat at the table. "I understand you've found your human family," Kristina said.

Kris looked down at his hands and nodded.

"Have you found your human mother?" Kristina asked.

Kris shook his head.

"I knew no mother would willingly give up a son as precious as you. But you did have a family. I was wrong to keep you."

"No you weren't." Kris looked Kristina in the eye. "Had you not taken me in I would have died. You gave me a good life."

"Your life has barely begun. You are still very, very young. Are you willing to leave the Glen forever?"

"I won't have to, Rule—"

"Yes, I know all about the Rules. I can hear Eldwin reading them as we speak. But there is still a great risk, despite your loophole. You may not know this, but there are many Elfs willing to help you, Eldwin included. If you fail, I will have lost both of my boys forever."

"I won't let you down. I can do this. I know I can."

"I hope so. Good luck. I'll be waiting for your return." Kristina reached up and kissed Kris on his cheek, and Kris hugged her in return, an embrace that outlasted the setting of the sun.

* * *

Word of Kris Kringle's departure spread through the Glen like brush fire, punctuated with cackles of laughter at the inanity of his goal and eventually doused with tears of sadness when the reality of the situation set in: Not only was Kris leaving, but two-dozen Elfs were going with him...much to the surprise of the High Council.

Haelan had been sure Kris would be alone in his quest to prove human virtue, but he did not consider how many Elfs would want to help Kris find his family. He certainly never imagined his own daughter would be one of the first to volunteer. By the end of the week the crew was prepared to embark on their journey to the top of the world.

The Elfs set forth, Kris in the lead. They pulled a large wagon loaded with tents and supplies, and each Elf carried a pack with clothes and bedding. They marched to the far northern border of the Glen, and beyond that to the edge of the sea.

"Do we have any boats?" Elaana asked Kris as the waves crashed over the rocks around them.

"Not yet," Kris said. "We need to thatch together a large raft. Then we can call on the whales and dolphins to help pull us across the sea."

They rolled up their sleeves and got to work. The prevalence of fallen timber made short work of the raft-building. They removed the wheels from the wagon and attached its body to the center of the raft and climbed aboard.

Indeed the animals of the seas were more than eager to help the Elfs, but Kris did not have the foresight to account for inclement weather. Not long after the shoreline had sunk beneath the horizon behind them a fierce wind arose and whipped the seas into a frenzy of mountainous waves, tipped with white froth and crashing over the Elfs, who clung to their raft with every ounce of strength they had.

The whales and dolphins pulled harder. When at last the storm abated the entire crew let up a cheer of relief to see the icy shores that lay ahead. They pried loose the wagon from the raft and attached a pair of skids to its bottom, transforming it into a snow-worthy sleigh. Kris stayed on board the raft until all the Elfs were safely on land. Then he took his first step onto the ice and snow.

"Ho-ho-ho!" Kris laughed. "My friends, soon we will find our new home, and once we are settled in the Great Northern Glen we can start to prepare for our first Christmas. I can't tell you how much I appreciate your help. We have much to do, and very little time to do it. But it will be worth it, in the end.

"During the journey across the sea, I was searching the hearts of the children of Oldenton, trying to find out which ones are my family."

"Did you find them?" Eldwin asked.

"I don't know yet if they are my relatives, but I did find a very special family. They are orphans, like me. A brother and sister, their names are Aaron and Alice, just lost their parents..." The Elfs shouldered their packs and began to forge a trail through the snow as Kris told them his tale.

CHAPTER 8
ORPHANS IN OLDENTON

It was the eve of Aaron's sixteenth birthday. Alice was only half his age. They were waiting for their parents to come home. Aaron and Alice waited up all night, but their parents never came. In the morning John Constable was the one who arrived to deliver the news: A wheel had fallen off their carriage and it crashed while they were riding along a high ridge. The carriage spilled over the edge, taking their parents with it.

It was a fall no human could survive.

Aaron celebrated his birthday at the cemetery. Uncle Horace pulled him aside once the last scoop of dirt settled on the graves. "You're a man now."

"That's what they say," Aaron said, his eyes on his father's grave.

"What do you say?"

Aaron looked up at his uncle. "I say I have no choice. I have a sister to look after and a business to run."

"A business to run. You plan to take over your father's mine, do you?"

"Do you?"

"We'll have to see what your father's will says. It will probably be one of us."

"We can't find his will. John Constable said that as his son, I am the legal owner unless someone can prove otherwise."

"Yes, you are that. The legal owner. For now."

"What do you mean by that?"

Uncle Horace said nothing more and walked away. Aaron sensed that a chasm had just opened between them, and although their common blood flowed in its depths, Uncle Horace had set fire to the bridge.

Aaron and Alice said goodbye to people as they left the cemetery—people who said they would help in any way, but in all reality they were people who had too many problems of their own to be able to deal with the needs of two orphans. Besides, Aaron was sixteen and a man, and he was expected to provide for his family.

Aaron and Alice walked home. They were offered rides, but neither wanted to sit in a wagon or carriage. In due time they found themselves snuggled in a pile of warm blankets in front of a roaring fire, trying to chase away the chill of the cemetery.

"Happy birthday," Alice said to her big brother. Aaron hugged her but said nothing. "What does it feel like to be a grown-up?"

Aaron looked down at her. His sister, now his ward; the burden of responsibility made for an uncomfortable yoke and Aaron had to clear a lump from his throat before he could speak.

"It feels heavier," he said. "It would feel different if Mom and Dad were still alive, I'm sure."

"They're still here. I can feel them," Alice said, and snuggled closer to her big brother, relishing his body heat.

I wish I could feel them, Aaron thought. "We'll be fine," he said. "As long as we have a warm house to sleep in and food for our bellies."

"And each other," Alice added.

"And each other."

Aaron watched the flames eat away at the wood in the fireplace. The old-timers said it was the coldest fall they could ever remember. They said it would only get worse as winter closed in. He had to gather more wood. And look after his sister. And run a coal mine.

Alice fell asleep in his arms as he watched the wood burn into embers and then extinguish into ash. The dark of night overtook the room but still he sat awake watching his future slowly arrive, second by second, and fearing each one upon the next. The light of day did not bring with it hope, but rather trepidation at the realities that he knew awaited him; realities that he had been sheltered from by virtue of childhood, but which would now be brought to full bear, faster than he could comprehend.

* * *

Aaron sharpened his axe. He hitched his mule to a pull-cart and headed off into the forest to collect firewood. Normally sweat poured off him when he chopped firewood, but not this time. The bitter wind forced its chill through his jacket and nipped at his hide.

The good, seasoned wood was gone. All that was left was fresh wood, most of it felled that summer. Fresh wood was wet, and wet wood would not burn easily; it would take a good amount of kindling to sustain a blaze. Aaron kept his eye out for kindling, but even the twigs and branches were few and far between.

The fresh trees were harder to chop, and when time finally came to head home, Aaron's cart was only half-full. A paltry amount to show for such a cold, hard day's work. And tomorrow he would have to go back to the mine, this time not as a miner-in-training but as its owner and manager.

On the road back to town he came upon his cousin Thomas pulling his own cart. Thomas was Uncle Horace's only child. Two years younger than Aaron, but also two inches taller, Thomas liked to throw his weight around. Even though they played together often as kids, Thomas had always been a bully, quick to dunk Aaron at the swimming hole. Thomas was also fond of a horrible human game where he would pin Aaron to the ground and straddle him, knees on arms, and dangle a spitball over his face. Thomas was usually very good about sucking the spitball back up before it actually broke free and splashed Aaron's cheeks, but he had his share of misses.

Thomas was especially mean to Alice. Once, when Alice was four and Thomas was ten, she convinced him to play dress-up with her. Uncle Horace beat Thomas when he saw his son in a skirt. Since then Thomas held a fierce grudge against Alice.

Aaron tried to hurry past him.

"Why isn't your sister with you? That mule will need to learn to manage her own load," Thomas said, sneering as Aaron went by.

"I could just use the jackass attached to your cart. Oh, wait. That's you."

"Say that again when I'm knighted and I'll run you through!"

"You? A knight? Fat chance! Knights are smart, brave, and courteous. Basically, they're everything you're not."

Thomas let go of the handle to his cart. "Knights are strong, and we fight for what is ours." He stepped closer to Aaron so their chests were almost touching.

"And what do you fight for, Thomas?"

"Whatever my father tells me. And when I leave my father, I will serve the king."

"That'll be a great day for our enemies. Get out of my way. I don't have time to deal with your nonsense. I have work to do."

Even Thomas's hot blood couldn't sustain a boil in the cold air. Aaron waited until Thomas stepped aside with a growl, then he trudged past. Thomas picked up the handles to his cart and followed.

CHAPTER 9

THE GREAT NORTHERN GLEN

The Elfs teamed together to pull the sleigh through the deep snow. Pots and pans clanged off the sides of the sleigh, their jingling lapsing in and out of rhythm as the Elfs sped up and slowed down, the disjointed melody accented by the bumps in the undulating ground. They passed many animals as they made their way farther north, and they noticed a curious change coming over familiar shapes. Fox and hare traded their traditional coats of red and brown for stark white fur. Enormous polar bears also wore coats that blended in with their snowy surroundings, as did the young seals they hunted.

The group marched on. The wind tried to halt their progress. Even the toughest human would have given up, and most men likely would have died, but the Elfs, being a stronger breed, were able to bear the cold, and Kris, with his half-Elf blood, was able to bear it right along with them...but not without side-effects.

It was Elaana who first noticed the strands of white creeping into his bushy red beard. "Your body seems to be quite taken in by the environment," she said.

"How so?" Kris asked.

"Look here," she pointed to a smooth patch of ice. Kris looked into it and squinted past the shine of the sun to see his reflection.

"Well I'll be," he said. Kris shook the snow off of his beard and ran his fingers through its length. The top layer was solid white, but the depths were still dark red.

"What are Aaron and Alice doing right now?" Elaana asked.

"I don't know. I have to concentrate to see them. Once we get settled I'll check in on them again."

The hills flattened out. The trees grew sparse as they passed the final remnants of land, then disappeared altogether as the Elfs made tracks over the frozen waters atop the Northern Ocean. The surroundings grew more and more desolate. As they neared the top of the world they advanced into the perpetual night of the northern winter. Several Elfs began to openly question their decision to leave their home. They complained that the Great Northern Glen was nowhere to be seen. Others noted that *nothing* was to be seen, and murmurs of regret laced the edges of all their conversations.

"Fear not, my friends," Kris said. "You acted in good will, and good will befall you."

"How do you know?" Eldwin asked.

"I can't say how I know, I just do. I know it like I know the sun will not rise here tomorrow."

"Supposing the Great Northern Glen did once exist. It was already a legend *ten-thousand years ago*! Look around you...there's no way it could still be here. This place is a wasteland!"

"Rule 10: *Kris Kringle may use the Great Northern Glen as his base camp.* The High Council agreed to this. They would not let you all come here in vain. They believe the Great Northern Glen exists. Haelan said this environment is needed to ensure its safety. We must carry on."

In time the group stopped and set up camp. They held a meeting in the main tent.

Kris stood in the middle of the crowd. "My friends," he said. "Thank you for joining me. There were many back home who thought we would never reach the sea, but look at how far we have come. And we will make it the rest of the way, fear you not. You have all shown a strength in body and mind that will be written about and remembered by Elfs for years to come. You, my friends, are the stuff legends are made of."

A cheer went up so strong the fabric of the tent flapped. "This camp is temporary. The Great Northern Glen *does* exist. You'll see."

"How soon?" asked one Elf.

"Where do you think it is?" asked another.

"I can't tell you that," Kris said. "But I know we will find it. Trust me. I'm a man of my word. Now for tonight...we celebrate!"

Kris clapped his hands and the Elfs burst into music and song, and brought forth bread and wine for dining. They sang for hours, and when they exhausted their traditional songs, the Elfs began to make up cheerful new songs recounting their journey, jingling bells to recall the sound of the pots and pans banging against the sleigh.

The sounds of their merry-making bounded across the ice, and a crowd of animals gathered round to witness the spectacle. Polar bear, fox, hawk, hare and seal all stood together in respectful silence, the spirit of the Elfs calming their wild nature so that none was threatened in the other's company.

When the final note of the last song faded into the wind, the Elfs emerged to an appreciative crowd. The air reverberated with roars and barks, squeaks and squawks as the animals all gave cheer in their native tongue. Kris stepped forward to speak.

"My friends, we need your help. We have come to stay, but do not wish to intrude. Our forefathers harbored a legend of a Great Northern Glen, a comfortable patch of trees sequestered away in the dense snow and ice. We need to find this Glen, for we know the trees within it will welcome us."

A large polar bear let out an affirmative roar and gestured with her head for Kris to follow. Kris and three young cubs scrambled after the mother bear as she ran off into the snow.

* * *

When Kris returned he stood before the Elfs in their main tent. He wore a somber expression, almost a scowl. "I have something to tell you about the Great Northern Glen."

Not an Elf said a word, but the air was abuzz with their thoughts. A consensus was quickly reached: The legend was wrong.

"The legend was wrong," Kris said.

"I knew it," Eldwin said. Kris held up his hand.

"The legend said the Great Northern Glen was a comfortable patch of trees." A broad smile lit up Kris's face. "But I tell you today it's a full-fledged forest! Wait till you see it! We need to pack up quickly, let's not waste time up here when our new home awaits us below."

Eldwin turned to Elaana. "Below?"

The Elfs packed up their tents and loaded the sleigh. Kris led them to a large crevice, with an easy slope meandering down into its dark-blue depths. The familiar jingle of pots and pans against the sideboards announced their entrance to the Great Northern Glen as the progression descended into the ice. The slope ran under the ice and leveled out into a long tunnel. A pinpoint of light in the distance gradually grew bigger. The tunnel floor was smooth; the pots and pans stopped their song. Their hush footsteps fell on a soft layer of snow.

The light surrounded them as they stepped out of the tunnel and into a grand cavern so big Eldwin swore he was back above ground. The light of the stars filtered in through tiny cracks in the surface ice, which amplified their rays and reflected them downward like mirrors. The ice at the top of the cavern glowed with the colors of sunset and the light emerged through pinholes in the ceiling like twinkling stars.

A thick grove of evergreen trees grew throughout the cavern, and at its front stood one large fir tree twice the size of the next tallest tree in the grove. Snow yielded to dirt topped with a soft covering of needles. In the distance, they heard the roar of a waterfall.

"Fir trees!" Eldwin exclaimed. He ran to the largest tree and climbed its branches to the very top. He rustled the tip like a father would his son's hair and looked out over the immense subterranean forest. Off in the distance he saw many fallen trees along a fissure, where a shift in the ice long ago weakened their roots. Plenty of wood to build with.

The Elfs stopped and watched Eldwin as he climbed down. He hugged the tree's trunk. His hands had no hope of ever clasping around it, even if he had ten other Elfs to help him make a chain.

"They've been waiting for us," he said.

The grand ice cavern soaked up all the *oohs* and *ahhs* as the Elfs explored their new home. The loudest noise did not echo, so vast was the chamber.

"This place is almost as big as the Woodland Glen," Elaana said. "It will take a year to explore it all."

"We can explore later. Christmas is only two moons away. The first thing we need to do is build houses, and then start on the toy factory," Kris said.

"There's plenty of fallen wood over there," Eldwin said, pointing. "I can't believe how big this place is. Who would ever believe that there's an entire forest buried under the snow, floating on top of the Northern Waters?"

"Hopefully nobody," Kris said. "We can't afford to be found, especially once our construction is complete. I'd hate to go through all this work for nothing."

"It sounds like you're setting up a permanent residence. Aren't you ever planning to leave and go back to the Glen? I thought that was the whole point, once you find your family," Elaana said.

"I plan to visit the Glen, and I expect Elfs to leave and others to come anew, but I plan to make this my home. I don't belong in the Woodland Glen, and I'm not sure if I belong in the world of the humans, either. But I *do* belong here. I can feel it."

"I'll stay here with you, as long as I can still visit the Glen," Elaana said.

Eldwin nodded. "Me too."

"I'm glad I have both of you here to help me. I'll need you to watch over things while I'm away."

"You're leaving so soon?" Elaana asked.

"I've got to start spreading the word to the children of Oldenton, to ask what they want for Christmas. Plus I need to get a feel for the human world. I can't just watch them in my head all the time."

"But what if a human sees you?" Eldwin asked.

"I can stay hidden while I can talk to them," Kris said. "I'll call down through the chimney."

"Good luck with that one," Eldwin said.

* * *

Eldwin' carpentry skills were put to good use. He and the other Elfs built a tidy little village near the base of the great tree, and around the tree's trunk they built their toy factory. The Elfs adorned the tree with the toys they carved while perfecting their craft. Every Elf gathered around the tree nightly, eager to sing, especially the new song with the jingling bells.

Every Elf was happy. Every Elf was safe. But for Kris, it was different. Kris knew the time had come for him to venture into the world of the humans.

CHAPTER 10
THE MOTHER LODE

Professor Hodgin stopped reading for a moment. All eyes were on him. No one spoke; even the wind outside was calm. Only the humming of the fan blowing over the ice core dared buffer the silence with its drone.

"No wonder Santa's village never showed up in the satellite images. It's under the ice," he said softly.

"Dad, how old do you think this book is?" Jason asked.

Professor Hodgin looked up. "I won't know until we study the core, but that will only tell us when the book was encased in the ice, not when it was written."

"I thought Santa Claus was just a myth. But this book proves he is real," Rebecca said.

Jason glanced out the window. The sunlight glinted off the snow with a new glow, adding a hint of warmth to the frigid landscape. "I knew it," he said. He wanted to take a picture of the book. He reached into his pocket for his camera, but it wasn't there. He had stopped carrying it days ago.

"How far away do you think the Great Northern Glen is?" Juan asked Professor Hodgin. "Do you think the crevice we found leads to the entrance?"

"I doubt it. You've peered over the edge. There's no slope, just a sheer drop...no way to get a sleigh through there."

"We should still check it out," Professor Nara said. "The Great Northern Glen must be close. For all we know, we're on top of it right now. I don't see how an area that big has avoided detection. We've all had subs under the Arctic ice."

"Maybe it has some property that allows it to absorb sonar, like a cloaking device," Rebecca said.

"Are these Elfs, or Klingons?" Juan asked.

"What climbing gear do we have?" Dan asked.

"Not enough to mount a serious expedition. We have picks and crampons, a couple hundred feet of rope, but only enough harnesses and carabiners for two climbers. I'm not sending anyone down there alone, and if we send two we have no equipment left for a rescue should anything go wrong. I'm not willing to accept that risk," Professor Hodgin said.

"Dad, we have to try," Jason said. "We can prove to the world that Santa Claus is real! If we don't do it now, someone else may beat us to it."

"Our names will go down in history," Rebecca said.

"And we'll be rich. We just hit the mother lode!" Juan said.

"Professor Hodgin, how much do you think this book it worth? A million dollars?" Rebecca asked.

"Way more," Professor Hodgin said. "That a book exists at all this deep in the ice is worth ten million. That it tells the history of Kris Kringle, ten times that."

"That it's written in magic ink that shows up in every language...priceless," Juan said.

"This book could fund our research for the next twenty years. We'll be able to go anywhere in the world to take samples. And we'll be self-funded, so we won't have to worry about some politician cherry-picking what data gets published," Professor Nara said. "Think about the possibilities. We have to find the Glen!"

"We already have the book. Our futures are secure in that. I'm not going to put anyone's life at risk to explore that crevice," Professor Hodgin said. "Not yet."

"Can we at least see what happens next?" Jason asked.

The team settled back as Professor Hodgin turned the page and continued reading.

CHAPTER 11

THE HUMAN WORLD

Kris left the Glen and headed south. Traveling alone was quicker than pulling a wagon with a team of Elfs. He moved fast, much faster than any man ever could. The cold wind of the Arctic night pulled on his hair and beard, stripping strand after strand of its hue and leaving a growing mane of silvery white in its wake.

The animals of the sea aided his crossing again, and this time the weather stayed at bay. When he reached the shores of the far continent, Kris set up camp and slept for two full days. After a quick breakfast he packed up and headed to Oldenton.

He made his way over a mountain and came to the edge of a steep cliff, ten times taller than the High Council's platform. Below he saw the sprawling hand of a forest, and in a clearing at its fingertips stood the town of Oldenton. Not a big town, certainly no human city, but comfortable for the families that lived there. A modest wall drew a thin line around the town. At its center, an inn and a tavern bustled at night and a marketplace thrived in the daytime. The

Smith, Miller, and Tailor families practiced their respective name-trades and dozens of other families farmed the land outside of town or worked in the coal mine up the valley.

Kris looked to his left and right. The cliff stretched on for hundreds of yards in each direction. He looked straight down.

"Why not?" he said to himself and stepped over the edge. At first he drifted down slowly. Half-way down he picked up speed. A lot of speed. Kris panicked as his coat flapped in the wind and the tops of the trees came fast to meet him. He grabbed at the branches to slow his fall and ended up with a stick in each hand when he crashed to the ground with a hefty thump.

"Oh. That's why."

Kris stood slowly and brushed himself off. He shouldered his pack and made his way through the woods to Oldenton.

Kris knew which house he would visit first. He found it at the edge of town. It was a good-sized house, two-stories and made of wattle and daub. It sat farther apart from its neighbors than they did from each other. Ivy tangled its way up a trellis from the ground to the rooftop along the back wall. As he approached, Kris stopped and closed his eyes, reaching out with his mind to see if anyone was home. He found Alice, dozing on a pile of furs in front of the fireplace as the orange embers sank into a deep pile of ash.

Kris looked to make sure no humans were out and about. It was still early. His cover of darkness was just the shadow of the mountain; the sky above carried the waning light of the evening sun and workers had not yet returned home from the fields or the mine. Kris floated up to the rooftop and hurried over to the chimney. He knelt next to it and called down.

"Alice, wake up. Can you hear me?"

Silence. Kris closed his eyes so he could watch her.

"Alice, wake—"

"Ahhhhhhhhhh!" Alice ran and hid behind the couch.

"Shhhhh. Please, don't be alarmed. I won't hurt you. Come to the chimney. I need to ask you something."

Alice peeked over the couch.

"Alice, don't be afraid." *This isn't anything like I thought it would be. Better just get to the point.* "Do you celebrate Christmas?"

Alice nodded.

"Good. I will come back on Christmas Eve, and if you leave a branch of an evergreen tree near the chimney, I will bring you a gift. What would you like me to bring?"

Alice scratched her head and thought. "A new pair of boots for my brother. His are too small, and he has to work in them every day. They hurt his feet something awful. I rub them for him sometimes, but sometimes that hurts more."

How can Haelan deny human virtue? This girl is selfless.

"Yes, of course, but what shall I bring for you?" he asked.

Alice rubbed her chin and thought some more. "A doll?"

Kris laughed. "Ho-ho-ho! Is that all? Come Christmas morning, you will find the most beautiful doll waiting for you."

"With fancy clothes," she added.

"Of course, what beautiful doll would be without them?"

"And a brush for her hair."

"Hair, yes. And a brush."

"And a horse-drawn carriage, with a driver and a bell. And—"

"What color horse?"

"You decide. Surprise me. Don't forget the brush."

"Of course not, I won't—"

"And she should have a house to sleep in, a grand house as beautiful as she is, with a big closet for all her fancy clothes and a soft bed for her to sleep in with a feather mattress and wool blankets and a cozy fireplace well stocked with wood so she doesn't catch cold and get sick but if she does she needs a kitchen so she can make soup to feel better because that's what Momma always did for me..."

The memory of her mother brought her to a halt.

Kris sat on the edge of the chimney with his feet inside it. He rested his elbow on his knees. "Alice, I know you've been a very good girl, and you are going through very bad times. I'll bring you your doll with her house and all her needs will be fulfilled. I just need you to put out the evergreen branch on Christmas Eve, okay?"

"Why?"

"Rule 53–A. If you leave the tree branch, I promise you I'll bring the grandest dollhouse you've ever seen!" Kris thrust his arms out wide like a Water Elf bragging about the size of the biggest fish under his care, but in his excitement he lost his balance and slipped down into the chimney. He landed on his feet at the bottom of the fireplace, his boots kicking up a cloud of embers and ash into the room.

"Is that you in the cinder clouds? Who are you?" Alice asked. She ran to the fireplace but before she got there Kris had risen back up the chimney and fled the house. He hated to think that he had already violated the Rules on his first foray into the world of the humans. This was going to be much harder than he thought. He hid behind a tree and closed his eyes, watching Alice in his mind.

Alice picked up a broom and dustpan and started to sweep up the fallen ash. She scooped up a glowing coal and tossed it back into the fireplace. When it landed she saw it settle right next to a pair of footprints. She leaned the broom against the wall and crouched down to study the footprints.

"Are you still there?" she called up the chimney. The only response was a faint echo of the wind, its rise and fall trickling down like the surf within a sea shell.

She watched the last of the embers extinguish, waiting for Aaron to come home so she could tell him. She heard the door creak and she leapt from the couch.

"Aaron! You won't believe what I saw! A man came in the cinder clouds, and he's going to bring us presents on Christmas!"

She stopped in her tracks when the door opened all the way and her cousin Thomas stood there, alone.

"Your stories get dumber as you get older. Some man named Cinder Clouds is bringing you presents? Ha! Fat chance." Thomas reached his hand out to move her aside and stepped into the foyer.

Alice slapped at his hand. "What are you doing here?"

"I'm checking out my new house."

"What? This is our house."

"Not for long. My father has a copy of your father's will. Turns out he left everything to us. You and Aaron get nothing."

"That's not true!"

"Oh, but it is. My father said a man from the King's court is coming to certify the will. And when we get the mine, we get this house too. You sure won't be able to afford it."

Thomas turned and walked away. Alice watched him tip his hat in greeting to someone unseen as he turned the corner. He stopped for a moment, said something Alice could not hear, and then hurried away.

Aaron came around the corner. When he saw Alice standing in the open doorway he quickened his pace.

"What did he want?" Aaron asked as he walked into his home.

"He's just a jerk."

"Tell me what he said to you."

"The same thing he always says. I hate him. He's always trying to start trouble. But something more important happened tonight. A man came in the cinder clouds."

"Cinder clouds? What are you talking about?"

Alice grabbed his hand and led him to the fireplace. "Look here, his boot prints!"

"Whose boot prints?" Aaron asked, kneeling down to inspect the ashen imprints.

"The man in the cinder clouds. I was sleeping on the couch and I heard a voice calling me through the chimney. He told me that he would bring us presents on Christmas, just like Mother and Father used to. All we have to do is lay out a branch from an evergreen tree on Christmas Eve. He's going to bring you a new pair of boots, and I'll get a new doll with a brush and a carriage and a house and—"

"You were dreaming," Aaron said.

"I was not dreaming. You see those footprints? Are you dreaming now?"

"I wish I was. I have bad news. There was an accident at the mine. Do you remember Davy Horner?"

"He's the head supervisor, right?"

"Not anymore. He fell down the shaft."

"But the shaft is so deep? How could he live?"

"He didn't."

They were both silent for a moment. Alice wrapped her skinny arms around her brother's sturdy waist. Aaron hugged her back.

"John Constable wants a hearing. Some people are claiming it was my fault for being a bad manager. They say I shouldn't be left in charge of the mine."

"Who are some people?"

"Uncle Horace, for one."

"What are you going to do?"

"I don't know. No one saw him fall. We all just heard his scream. It was terrible."

"What's that on your neck?" Alice reached up and touched her finger to a spot just below her brother's left ear. A sticky wetness clung to her fingertip.

Aaron reached his own hand up and felt the spot of blood. He stared at his hand.

"Are you hurt?" Alice asked.

"No. This isn't my blood." He ran his fingers through his hair, knowing now that his sweat only made up part of the dampness he felt. "I need to draw a bath," he said as he peeled off his shirt.

CHAPTER 12
A NARROW ESCAPE

Kris sat in a tree just outside the gates to the town, watching as Aaron kneeled over the washbasin and doused his head under the cold well-water. Alice offered to heat it for him, but he would not wait.

A sound startled Kris and his eyes fluttered open. Over the howling wind he heard two riders approaching. Kris moved fast, climbing the tree to its top branches to keep from being seen.

The riders spoke, their words carried upward on the wind to the high boughs where Kris kept hidden.

"Davy would still be alive if the mine were run by an adult."

"True. It's tragic that Richard Miner passed on, but young Aaron has no business trying to take his place."

"What will we do without coal? Think about what will happen if they halt production."

"Our market will die, for starters. Half the wares sold are to people who come from afar to buy coal."

"There's already a shortage of seasoned wood, and we're on the verge of the worst winter in our lifetimes. Without coal to fuel our kitchens and warm our houses…"

Kris watched the men ride through the gates, into the town and out of earshot. He recognized one of them as Aaron's Uncle Horace. Confident he could stay hidden and intent to hone his listening skills, Kris scurried down the tree and ran to the town wall, a ten-foot high stone structure with wooden ramparts positioned along its top. He jumped over the wall with ease, touching down silently on a gravel path. To his right, the main road, cobblestones interspersed with hard-packed earth. To his left the path disappeared between two buildings.

Kris entered the dark alley between the buildings, his eyes rivaling those of a cat in their ability to quickly adapt to the low light. Two rats stared at him with contempt and guarded the scraps they dined upon.

Kris continued down the alley. The sound of horse hooves clopping on the cobblestone road tethered him to his target. The hoof-beats stopped in front of the tavern in the center of town. The two riders dismounted, hitched their horses, and cozied up to a small table on the side of the room near the window.

Kris could see them through the window, but even his finely tuned Elfin ears could not pick up their conversation over the din inside the tavern: A mandolin played while a group of young men sang far-fetched tales of a recent battle; an old man ranted loudly about politics to all who could hear him; the barmaid spread gossip from table to table, dropping bits of one conversation into another, her rumors melting into the crowd like fresh butter on a warm muffin.

Kris crouched under the eaves of a locked doorway and closed his eyes so he could reach out with his mind. Kris knew his actions were reckless: Even though his only present company was a pair of rats, the risk remained that someone could come through the alley any moment. With his eyes shut and his attention focused on the conversation inside the bar, he would be oblivious to the intruder. At the risk of discovery—which would lead to a life of exile from the Glen, for him and every Elf who had accompanied him— Kris picked back up on the conversation.

The two men were surprisingly candid, the noise of the room providing ample distance from any wandering ears, especially those of the bar maiden, whom they knew to look out for in any regard.

"I found an old draft of my brother's will, from before his children were born. It names me as beneficiary. The mine. All mine. My mine."

"How can you be so sure?"

"I have an...acquaintance. Someone in the king's court. He's coming to town to review the will, and I fully expect that he will certify it with the regal authority he represents. Once he does, no one will be able to contest me."

"Unless the real will shows up."

"I'm not worried about that. Last year my brother drafted a new will, but nobody will ever find it."

"Where is it?"

"Gone forever."

"How can you be so sure?"

"My brother had it with him the night he died. I believe he was off to register it. I found it in a box halfway up the hillside after the crash, it must have been thrown from the carriage. Needless to say, both the box and the will it contained no longer exist."

A noise snapped Kris' eyes open and he saw two men stagger into the alley. They had come from the tavern, and the men, arms around each other's shoulders and singing a song to which neither knew the words, failed miserably at walking a straight path through the alley. Kris pulled his hood down over his face and curled up against the door, pretending to sleep. The two men passed him without taking notice.

The close encounter left Kris badly shaken, and once the men were out of sight he back-tracked to the town wall and left for the safety of the forest.

Once he was comfortable within the shelter of the trees, Kris sat back down to resume his people-watching. It took him some time to find Horace again, and by the time he did, he could see the man lying in bed, drifting off to sleep and dreaming of the riches he would soon inherit. Kris took advantage of the opportunity to get some much-needed sleep himself.

When he finally awoke, the sun was already high in the sky, past its mid-day peak and starting its trek to the western horizon. Kris stood and stretched and brushed the leaves and dirt from his clothes. He took a few bites from a loaf of bread in his pack and let the sounds of a bubbling brook guide him to a refreshing drink of water.

Aaron and Alice remained at the forefront of his thoughts. Horace and his son Thomas seemed to epitomize everything Haelan ever said about humans, particularly their greed and their willingness to hurt others, even those in their own family. Instead of finding virtue, Kris found himself face-to-face with treachery, corruption, and greed. His proof of virtue would be elusive, but he was determined to find it.

CHAPTER 13

A HELPING...PAW?

Back at the Great Northern Glen, the Elfs continued to prepare for Christmas. So much had to be done. The old wagon had to be torn apart and re-built into a sleek and sturdy sleigh. Eldwin's carpentry skills were put to good use with that task, but in his quest for perfection building the sleigh Eldwin had no time to help with anything else.

Elaana knew the Elfs wouldn't be able to pull the sleigh for Kris, so she sought volunteers among the animals. The polar bears proved to be too slow; they could run fast for short distances, but could not keep pace long enough for Kris to make his rounds in one evening. The Arctic hares had tremendous speed, but even Eldwin's greatest engineering could not produce a sleigh light enough for them to pull.

Elaana was desperate for a solution. The larger beasts of the southern lands—oxen, horses, and the like—could not survive in the frigid north. One day, while walking deep in the woods of the Great Northern Glen, her hope teetering on the brink of exhaustion, she came upon an Arctic fox.

"Can you help me?" she pleaded.

The fox turned to her and perked up its ears. "It depends on what you need," the fox said.

"I need to move something."

"Where is it?"

"Here in the Great Northern Glen."

"Where do you need to move it to?"

"The northern lands of the humans."

The fox let out a low growl.

"And back."

"I can't help you," the fox said. "No fox will willingly go near the humans. But I know who will."

"Who?" Elaana asked.

"My cousins, the dogs. They're strong, and they love the humans for some dumb reason. Obedient, strong, but not too bright. So what is it you need to move, anyway?"

"A sleigh."

"That's like a sled, right?"

"Yes, it's a large sled."

"That's no problem. Dogs pull sleds for the humans all the time, it's in their blood. You'll need a team of them. Watch out, though. They don't always get along with each other. And they aren't intelligent, like we are. They are more brawn than brain," the fox cautioned.

"I'll keep that in mind, thank you. Where are they?"

"There's a pack of them roaming this Glen. Finding them should be easy. You can usually attract them by whistling. Or bring food."

"What do they eat?" Elaana asked.

"Any kind of meat or bones will do. Or cat poop. The dogs are quite indiscriminate in their diets, and they can smell disgusting things from a great distance."

"Thank you. Is there anything I can do to repay you your kindness?"

"Just keep the humans away."

"Don't worry," Elaana said. "We don't want the humans here anymore than you do."

Elaana went back to the toy factory and found four volunteers to help her go out and round up a team of sled dogs.

CHAPTER 14
A CHANGE OF HEART

Professor Hodgin stopped reading and cleared his throat. "Sled dogs. I didn't see that one coming."

"Maybe the magic English translator is broken," Jason said. "Everyone knows Santa uses reindeer to pull his sleigh."

"It says dogs in Japanese," Professor Nara said.

"Spanish, too," Juan said.

"The fox referred to its cousins. That has to be dogs," Rebecca said.

"Professor Hodgin, we haven't done any local recon since we found the crevice," Dan said. "What if the entrance to the Glen is nearby? Our crevice may not lead to it, but there's one somewhere that does," Dan said. "I can fire up Blackbird and look around."

"That's not a bad idea," Professor Hodgin said. "Go see what you can find."

"Will do. I'll suit up and get a move on," Dan said.

"We'll keep a radio on in here, let us know immediately if you find something."

"Professor?" Dan asked. Professor Hodgin looked up at him. "You mind reading into that radio?"

"Can't wait to hear what happens next, can you?" Juan asked.

"Well...no. But still, there might be clues, you know, landmarks I could look for or something."

"Roger that," Professor Hodgin said. "We'll make sure you hear every word."

Dan hurried out of the lab.

"Dad, what will we do if he finds the entrance to the Great Northern Glen? I mean, do we knock on the door and ask for Mr. Kringle?"

"I'm not sure, Jason. I don't think it's going to be that easy to find. Who knows, Santa might just see us coming and welcome us with open arms."

"But what if he doesn't?" Jason asked. "In the book, it says they don't want to be found. What if us finding them violates a Rule?"

"*Us* finding *them* doesn't, from the Rules we know about."

"But we don't know them all, do we?"

"Well, no..."

"So we can't do it. You should call Dan back."

"Jason, you're the one who wanted to come here to take a picture of Santa. Now you may actually get that chance, and you want to let it pass by? There's no guarantee you will ever have the opportunity again."

"I don't think we're supposed to find him."

"I think you're rushing to judgment. Why don't we finish the book, and then we'll decide what we'll do when we find the Glen, okay?"

"Okay."

CHAPTER 15
THE MAN IN THE CINDER CLOUDS

Kris had planned on visiting each child in Oldenton to tell them he was coming on Christmas. He never guessed Alice would do it for him.

Alice was an exceptional gossip. She told anyone and everyone that the man in the cinder clouds was coming to town to bring presents on Christmas day. She relayed the news with such excitement that people often had trouble understanding the rapid succession of words spilling from her mouth. In turn, they thought Cinder Clouds was the man's name. It stuck.

Kris watched in his mind as the word spread, and the children of the town talked excitedly about the gifts Cinder Clouds would bring them. Over the next several nights he went back into town, and speaking to children through chimneys and bedroom windows he collected their requests. He also made sure each child was clear on the most important Rule (for them): they had to set an evergreen branch near the fireplace on Christmas Eve. No branch, no gift. No exceptions.

Out of all the children in Oldenton, Kris found only one who did not ask for a gift: Thomas. It started with his stubborn refusal to believe Alice when she asked her cousin what he would wish for when Cinder Clouds came.

"I'm going to be a knight someday, and knights don't play silly games. Cinder Clouds is make-believe. Nobody will bring you presents on Christmas. Your parents used to, and my father might have if you and your brother weren't so bothersome. But now, you'll get nothing. And your brother will get thrown in jail for killing Davy Horner. Then you'll have to go live in an orphanage."

"That's not true! It was an accident. Aaron was down in the mine when Davy fell, he wasn't anywhere near him."

"He should have been. If Aaron had been where he was supposed to be, Davy wouldn't have fallen. If anyone should have fallen, it should have been your stupid brother."

Alice swung her arm to slap Thomas but he grabbed her wrist before she made contact. He let go and pushed her to the ground.

"Stupid little girl," he said.

Alice glared at Thomas as she scrambled to her feet. "You'll see," she said. "I know Cinder Clouds is real. I don't care what you say or what you wish for. I know I'm going to get a present next to my evergreen branch."

"Come Christmas, you won't have an evergreen branch *or* a present," Thomas said and walked away.

Even after that encounter, Kris had tried to ask Thomas what he wanted. The Rules said that he had to bring a gift to each child in Oldenton. But Thomas' disbelief made the boy deaf to his voice, and Kris could never get his attention.

Kris made a list with the other children's names and the gift each wanted most. Toys and candy dominated the list. He checked over his list—twice—before leaving town to head back to the Great Northern Glen.

He stopped to nap under a tree before crossing the waters. It was an unusually warm afternoon, so he took off his coat and used it as a pillow. A loud thrashing woke him; a deer ran by, followed by a hunter. Kris barely got away undetected. He left in such a hurry he forgot his coat and his pack of provisions.

Kris made his way north. The temperature dipped and the polar winds thrashed at him. He regretted losing his coat. The Arctic air chilled him to his core. Without insulation or food his Elfin strength began to fail him. Kris struggled with each step. He rubbed his hands up and down his shivering arms to keep warm. Trudging through the snow and ice was hard work, and sweat froze to his forehead as he pushed himself to the limit, and beyond.

By the time he reached the final mile to the Great Northern Glen his hair and beard were caked with ice and snow. His clothes dangled like rags, his muscular frame depleted by the strenuous walk across the Arctic wasteland. He tried to carry on, but the final push proved too much and Kris collapsed in the snow.

* * *

Elaana hitched the dogs to the sleigh. The unruly pack of canines sniffed the harness. They sniffed the snow. They sniffed each other's butts. They growled and howled. Elaana shook the reins and hollered "Mush!" The dogs raced forward. Elaana's feet went out from under her and she tumbled over into the backseat of the sleigh as it sped up the ramp and out of the Glen. The moon and the multitude of stars illuminated the ice and snow.

Elaana climbed back to the front seat and pulled on the reins, steering the dogs first right then left. She made wide loops and figure-eights, sending up rooster-tails of snow as she carved tracks through the ice.

She was preparing for a final pass around the perimeter when something caught her eye. Elaana steered closer and then pulled back on the reins to slow the dogs.

"Halt!" Elaana yelled at the top of her lungs and yanked on the reins as hard as she could. The dogs ground to a halt. Elaana jumped from the sleigh and ran to a snow drift. It was not the drift that caught her attention, it was the boot sticking out of it.

Kris' boot.

CHAPTER 16
DECEPTION, TREACHERY, & GREED

Buried in the snow, unable to move, Kris drifted off into a deep trance. His mind wandered to the same place it always did—the minds of humans. What he saw made him want to shake his fist in anger, but he was frozen solid. He didn't even have enough control to force his mind to look away. Powerless, he watched the treachery unfold.

Horace called a meeting of all the merchants and craftsmen in town. John Constable was there, too, along with Count Whitley, officiating on behalf of the King's court. Horace wasn't taking any chances. He wanted the ruling to be as official as possible.

"My friends, the loss of Richard and Elise Miner was indeed tragic. Not only was Richard a great businessman, and friend to everyone in town, he was my brother. My heart still aches from the loss we all share. My heart aches further at the loss of Davy Horner, and for his wife and children. The worst part is that Davy's life could have been spared had the mine been under proper management, and I fear Davy's life will not be the last one lost unless we correct this situation. Simply put, Aaron Miner is too young and lacks the experience needed to run the mine."

John Constable spoke up. "Aaron Miner is the rightful heir. As Richard Miner's son, and now officially an adult, he holds title to the land and the coal under it."

"I have documents that prove otherwise," Horace said. He held aloft a leather-bound parchment. "My brother left a will."

"Bring it forward," said Count Whitley. Horace handed him the documents. He took his time reading it, holding it up to the light to scrutinize the wax seal and the officiating signature before decreeing it legally binding and wholly legitimate.

"That's fine, but what does it say?" asked Jon Miller.

Count Whitley cleared his throat. "I, Richard Miner, do hereby bequeath upon my passing, my home and the land on which it sits, and the mine and the land upon which it sits, to my wife, Elise.

"Should Elise join me in my passing, or pass on before me, then all of my properties and possessions shall be transferred to the ownership of my brother, Horace Farmer."

Count Whitley folded the leather cover closed and looked out upon a sea of incredulous stares.

It was Timothy Wooler who spoke first. "I don't believe it. What's the date on that thing? I haven't seen you and your brother exchange a kind word to each other in a dozen years. Why would he leave you anything, let alone everything?"

"This document has been ratified as legal by decree of the court of the King," Count Whitley said. "I will not entertain further debate on the subject."

Horace held up a hand toward Count Whitley.

"Please," he asked. "I can explain."

Horace walked to the center of the room and stood among the crowd. Skeptical glares pierced him from all sides, but Horace did not waver in his confidence as he spoke.

"Yes, it's true that my brother and I often seemed at odds, but I assure you the differences we had were superficial. They did not reach our families. My brother always knew that I would look after his children should tragedy befall him and Elise. I have a will that says the same for him, although come to think of it, I need to update it. It's easy to forget such things, you know.

"You may remember many of our quarrels, some of which were public, to our mutual embarrassment. But know this: I loved my brother, and we had between us a bond of blood that was never broken.

"When our father passed away, my brother and I both received land. It is land that our father inherited from his father. Land that has been in our family for generations. It is the will of our forefathers that the land not leave our family, and my brother understood that above all else."

"Then why leave it to you and not his son?" Andrew Smith asked.

"Aaron is a fine lad, but he is not ready to manage the property. A sad fact, but Davy Horner's widow can attest to it."

Murmurs rose above the crowd and filled the air under the ceiling. Count Whitley stood to speak, but Horace gave him a glance that made him stop. The murmurs quieted.

John Constable walked to the front of the room. "Stanger things have happened, although this is quite high on the list. Were it not for Count Whitley—the honorable representative of the King—to certify these documents, many of us would cry foul. But as it stands, the Last Will and Testament of Richard Miner has been ratified as legal and binding. We all must honor its authenticity."

"I'm certain my brother and his wife both appreciate your prudence in this matter, God rest their souls," Horace said.

"This meeting is concluded then," Count Whitley said. "Any further disputes on this matter shall be handled in the King's own court. I bid you all farewell."

* * *

Horace mounted his horse and rode it at a canter down the South Road, away from town and toward his farm. Once he was out of sight from the town walls, he steered off the road and worked his way through the woods to the East Road, stopping behind a tall thicket before he reached the road itself.

Two travelers passed by on foot, heading into town. A moment later, the carriage carrying Count Whitley came down the road.

"Stop for a moment," Count Whitley told the driver. "Nature calls."

Horace looked through the branches as the carriage rolled to a stop right in front of him. Count Whitley climbed down and walked around the bush to Horace. He held a finger to his lips and extended his other hand. Horace handed him a sack, careful not to jingle the coins inside. Count Whitley tied the sack to his belt and hid it under his cloak. Horace backed away silently and stole away into the night as Count Whitley climbed back into his carriage and sped away.

* * *

The next day, Aaron woke early and headed off to the mine on his horse. He had called a meeting of all the workers. He wanted to discuss the safety procedures to make sure an accident like Davy Horner's didn't happen again.

Aaron stabled his horse and walked into the mess hall, a wooden pavilion with a low ceiling and no walls. Tables and benches black with coal dust sat in rows on the dirt floor. A circular fireplace stood in the center of the pavilion, above it a hood and chimney dropped from the ceiling like an upside-down funnel. Horace was sitting on the edge of the fireplace, stirring the remaining coals from the prior evening's fire with a stick.

"You're here early," Aaron said.

"We have important matters to attend to today."

"I know, I called the meeting."

"Yes, yes. You did do that, didn't you? But there are more urgent topics for discussion than your belated speech on safety."

"What are you talking about?" Aaron asked.

"You should already know, but for some reason you didn't come to last night's meeting of the Council of Merchants."

"I had to go home to look after my sister."

"A lot of responsibility you have these days, eh? Well, let me fill you in. A representative from the King's court, Count Whitley, attended and ratified your father's will."

"My father's will? It's been found?"

"Oh, yes. It's been found. Unfortunately for Davy Horner it was found too late. But now that the mine is under my control—"

"What?"

"—we shan't be having any more accidents of that nature." Horace folded his arms across his chest and watched the corners of his nephew's mouth drop. Aaron's eyes glistened and his bottom lip quivered, then the boy stood straight and clenched his fists at his side.

"My father would not have given you the mine. Ever. The will is fake—"

"The will has been ratified by the King's court. If you wish to dispute it, you need to argue your case there, not here."

"Whatever treachery put the title of the mine in your filthy hands will be undone. Mark my words."

Horace glanced around to make sure they were alone. He stepped closer to Aaron and lowered his face so close Aaron could taste the onions on his breath when he spoke. "Now look here, you little knave. Treachery put the land in your father's hands to begin with. He never told you about *his* inheritance, did he?"

Aaron shook his head.

"I wouldn't think so. *I* was the elder son. But because your grandfather married my mother after my real father died, I was not his blood. When your grandfather died, he left me nothing. Your father got it all. I was twenty years old. Your father was only ten. Who do you think ran the mine until your father was of age? Me. That's who. And when your father was finally able to take over—and he was three years older than you are now when he did—how did he repay me? By granting me a stinking pig farm!"

Horace spat on the ground, narrowly missing Aaron's boot.

"So now you steal it from me, after I lost my father."

"I lost *two* fathers! And I got nothing out of it. I had to work for my living. Now you will, too. You can't collect on any money from this mine without going through me, by order of the King's law. And you can't work here anymore, either. Your performance has been unsatisfactory, to say the least."

"You have no right!" Aaron yelled.

"On the contrary, I have every right. At long last. Now run along...go find your sister and play dress-up. We men have work to do here."

Aaron walked over to his horse, but Horace stopped him. "That animal is property of this mine."

"How will I get home?"

"What, are your legs broken?"

"Are you suggesting I walk?"

"Oh, you *are* a bright one. Yes. Walk." Horace waved him off. "Toodle-oo."

Horace grinned but said nothing further. Aaron left, passing the other miners as they began to arrive. They saw the expression on his face and looked at each other with raised eyebrows.

When they saw Horace standing in the pavilion with his wicked grin they knew that all of their lives had just gotten much more difficult.

CHAPTER 17
TRAPPED IN HIGH PLACES

A knock on the door woke Alice. She climbed out of bed and put on her robe. The knocking came again, louder.

"Who is it?" she yelled against the door.

"Open up."

Thomas. Alice pulled a chair over and stood on it to open the tiny door that served as a peephole. Her cousin's snarling face greeted her.

"I have an eviction notice."

"What does that mean? Are you playing another one of your dumb knight-games?"

Thomas held a paper to the peephole. "Read it and weep. You can't live here anymore, this house is the property of the mine, and the King's court has declared my father its legal owner. He sent me to tell you to leave this house."

"Make me," Alice said and stuck her tongue out. Then she closed the peephole.

"You little…" The doorknob shook. Alice's smiled faded when she heard the sound of a key inside the lock. The tumblers clicked as the key turned and the lock yielded. Alice gasped when the door swung open, its handle denting the wall where it hit. The chair she had been standing on ran across the room as if its legs were alive.

Thomas chased after Alice, who ran to the far side of the kitchen table. Thomas circled the table to catch her, but she was quick enough to keep to the opposite side. Frustrated, Thomas pushed the table with all his might, using it to pin Alice to the wall behind her.

"Ouch! You're hurting me," Alice said.

"That's what you get. You should have done what you were told. I was going to give you a week, but I changed my mind. Get out. Now." Thomas pulled the table back and Alice fell to the floor.

"Get up." Thomas stood over her. She didn't move.

Thomas reached down to pick Alice up. She grabbed his arm and bit his hand at the base of his thumb. Thomas yelped and pulled his hand back. Her jaws held firm enough that he stood her up in the process. She let go and Thomas grabbed her arms at the wrists. He dodged several wild kicks as he turned her around and marched her out the front door, giving a final push as they crossed the threshold, sending Alice spilling onto the cold, hard ground.

Thomas pulled the door closed behind him and locked it. He turned to Alice, tipped his hat with his bloody hand, and whistled as he walked away.

Alice stood. The rocks in the dirt poked her bare feet. She pulled her robe close around her and walked to the porch. She tried the door, even though she knew she would not be able to open it. All of the windows were closed and locked as well. *If only I could come through the chimney, like Cinder Clouds...*

Alice walked to the back of the house and eyed the trellis laced with ivy that ran up the siding, all the way to the roof. She began to climb.

* * *

Aaron walked along the road back to Oldenton, a trip that took nearly an hour by horse. He neared the halfway-point when a noise off in the brush caught his attention. A wolf stared at him through the foliage. Aaron gripped the handle on his knife and drew it from its sheath. It was just an all-purpose work knife, dull from repeated use, but it would have to do. At least the wolf stood alone.

Aaron continued slowly down the road, turning so that he still faced the wolf as he walked backwards. The wolf stepped out of the brush and onto the road. Another followed behind it. And another.

Aaron turned and sprinted, barks and growls coming close behind him. He saw a tree with low branches and ran to it. He put his knife in his mouth and leapt through the air, grabbing a branch with both hands. He lifted one leg over the branch and hooked his foot in where the branch met the tree trunk. He was pulling his other leg up when a wolf sank its teeth into his calf.

Aaron screamed and almost lost his grip as the pain shot through his body. His ankle grew wet and warm. He grabbed the knife from his mouth and swung his hand down. The animal let go of his leg and howled. Aaron lost his grip on the handle as the wolf fell to the ground, his knife still in its side.

Aaron clambered up the tree as the other two wolves circled its base. They nuzzled their wounded companion and howled in unison. Their howls were matched far off into the woods, at least four more wolves responding to the call. The wolves continued to call back and forth, the remote ones sounding closer with each subsequent round.

Aaron ripped a sleeve from his shirt and tied it around the wound on his leg. He held onto the tree and waited for rescue; when or how that might happen, he had no idea.

* * *

Alice climbed the trellis, careful not to slip and fall. As she reached for the edge of the roof, the cross-beam under her left foot snapped. She lost her balance and started to fall. With both hands she clawed at the trellis, pulling away the ivy that twisted around it like ribbons on a fancy gift.

Her hands finding no secure surface, she turned and fell, but the drop was quickly arrested as her robe snagged on the broken board where she had been standing. Alice hung dangling high above the ground, looking down at a distance she did not want to descend by force of gravity alone. Her back against the trellis, she tried to get a grip or find a secure footing, but the second she moved she heard a ripping sound within the garment acting as her life-line. Paralyzed with fear, she stayed as still as she could, her breath coming rapidly in short gasps as she prayed for her brother to come home and help her.

CHAPTER 18
A DARING RESCUE ATTEMPT

Kris opened his eyes. "We have to go now," he said, not knowing where he was or to whom he was speaking. He tried to sit up but someone held him down.

"Be still," Elaana's voice soothed him. Her words had the opposite effect. "You're not going anywhere. You've been unconscious for two days, after being frozen in a snow drift for who-knows-how-long. Now you wake up all of a sudden and demand to leave. Do you even know where you are?"

"The Great Northern Glen?" Kris asked.

"That's a good start. What year is it?"

"51,413 by the Elfin calendar."

"The old calendar or the new calendar?"

"What do you mean? There's only one calendar."

"Okay, good enough. Sit up." She patted the top of his head.

Kris sat up, and as he did he caught a glimpse of himself in the mirror over the dresser. His hair was completely white, as was his beard.

"My red is gone." Kris ran his fingers through his hair. "All of it."

Kris swung his legs over the side of the bed. They stuck out from his body like toothpicks. A cough rattled his chest. He rubbed his side, surprised to feel his ribs so prominently through his skin.

"My word, I'm just a sack of bones." He shivered. "It's freezing in here."

"We need to fatten you up, that'll keep you warm. Here, start with this." Elaana handed Kris a bowl of soup and a loaf of bread.

"We really need to go," Kris said through a mouthful of broth-laden bread. He swallowed. "Aaron and Alice are in trouble. This is a matter of life or death!"

"You can't go anywhere. You're not immortal, Kris. Do you realize how close you just came to finding that out?"

Kris explained the situation to Elaana while he finished his meal (and seconds...and thirds). He knew he couldn't make the trek back to Oldenton by foot, especially given the speed at which he would need to travel.

"We have to do something," Kris said as Elaana placed the empty bowl on a tray. "Is the sleigh ready?"

"The sleigh is, but the dogs aren't passing the speed tests we'll need for Christmas...let alone an emergency rescue in two places at once. They can hardly go a mile without stopping to pee on something."

"There has to be another way," Kris said as he put on his boots. He stood up on shaky legs and sat back down. With his elbows on his knees he cradled his head in his hands and closed his eyes tight.

"I can see them both right now. Aaron's leg is sure to get infected, and those wolves are still there, drooling. Alice is hanging from the trellis in the cold, in bare feet and a nightgown. She won't survive the nighttime temperatures. That's assuming she doesn't fall first."

Kris took a deep breath and stood back up, swaying like a tree in the breeze for a moment before getting his balance.

"Get back in bed. I'll go look for them," Elaana said.

"You can't. That's a violation of the Rules."

"Which one?"

"Rule 1,845. I'm the only one who's allowed to go to Oldenton."

"You aren't thinking clearly. We're three days away from Christmas. Luckily I found your list tucked inside your shirt. Eldwin and his crew are working on the toys. We have too much to do here to be ready, we can't spare the time."

"What if they are my family? Out of all the children in Oldenton, I feel the strongest connection with Aaron and Alice. I have to help them."

"It's too risky. They'll see you, and if they do and the High Council finds out they will surely banish you for life, loophole or not. I don't think I can help you with my father then."

"Then help me now. I need you. Aaron and Alice need you."

"This isn't just about them. Or you. We'll be putting every Elf up here at risk."

"If you stay here, fine, I understand. But please don't try to stop me."

"Kris, wait..." Elaana followed Kris as he crossed the Glen to the building where the sleigh was parked. Kris stared at the dog harnesses, clueless as to how they worked. Elaana opened the door to the kennel and whistled. The dogs rushed out at once, looking like one giant ball of fur. They yipped and yapped and lapped at Kris's cheeks.

"Ho-ho-ho! How can you not love dogs? Man's best friend indeed! Are you ready to pull the sleigh?" He scratched one behind its ears.

The dogs wagged their tails and barked, as dogs are prone to do. But when Kris tried to put their harnesses on, they told him in no uncertain terms that they were done with the sleigh for the day.

"Let me try," Elaana said. She struggled but eventually hitched every dog up.

Kris and Elaana climbed on to the sled, and Elaana yelled, "Mush!"

The dogs didn't move.

Kris yelled, "Mush!"

The dogs turned around and barked.

"Hmph. Man's best friend, indeed."

Elaana shook the reins and yelled again. The dogs moved forward slowly, but stopped at the door. A low growl started on one dog's throat, then another's. Then, without warning, they darted forward into the Glen.

The sleigh rocked side to side on its runners as the dogs turned sharp corners around trees. Elaana and Kris both pulled back on the reins and called for the dogs to halt, but the dogs barked and ran on, chasing an Arctic hare.

Kris and Elaana held on for dear life as the dogs raced through the trees and along the banks of the Great Northern Glen's mighty Meltwater River. Eventually the hare escaped into a tunnel. The dogs tried to dig after it, but soon gave up. They looked back at Elaana and Kris and cocked their heads to the side, as if to say, *Okay, that was fun. What do you want to do now?*

"Where are we?" Elaana asked.

"Beats me. I haven't been this far into the Glen before. I had no idea it was this big."

They climbed out of the sleigh and inspected it. A couple scratches, but no major damage. "Eldwin sure is one good carpenter. This thing is tough," Elaana said.

Kris scratched his head and looked around. He tried to follow the sleigh tracks backwards to see what direction they had come from, but the tracks looped around trees and criss-crossed over each other. It was impossible.

"We're lost. We'll never make it in time now. I can't believe this is happening." Kris climbed into the sleigh and slumped down in the front seat. He covered his face with his hands.

The sound of rustling leaves drifted through the Glen.

"What's that?" Elaana asked.

The dogs sniffed the air. They let out a couple yips, unsure of the scent they were picking up.

The sound continued, getting closer. Kris climbed down from the sleigh. "Hello?" he called.

Out of the woods stepped two reindeer.

"Well, I'll be," Kris said. "They must live in here. Sorry to intrude, friends, we were brought here by accident. Can you help us get back home?"

The reindeer nodded. "Are you the one called Kris Kringle?" one of them asked.

"I am," Kris replied.

"You are known throughout this Glen. We would be glad to help. I am Donder, and this is Blitzen. What can we do for you?"

"Can you train dogs to pull a sleigh properly?" Elaana asked.

"I think we can do better than that. Let your dogs go. We'll pull your sleigh," Blitzen said. The dogs sniffed each other, indifferent to their pending unemployment.

"But there are eight dogs, and only two of you," Kris said. Six more reindeer stepped out from behind the trees. "We could all use a little excitement," Donder said. "Life in the Glen isn't bad, but our reindeer games do get monotonous after a while."

Elaana unhitched the dogs, who disappeared into the woods in pursuit of trees to pee on. The reindeer lined up and waited patiently as Kris and Elaana hitched them up, introducing themselves in the process. Dasher and Dancer paired up at the front of the line, followed by Prancer and Vixen, then Comet and Cupid. Donder and Blitzen took the positions closest to the sleigh.

"Are you sure you don't mind?" Kris asked as he and Elaana settled into the sleigh.

"Come on team, let's show them what we can do," Blitzen said, and the reindeer took off.

The force of the acceleration pushed Kris and Elaana back into the cushions of the seat, and trees whipped past them in a blur. Kris looked ahead and saw a large tree branch stretching over the path in front of them. There was no way they could clear it. It would surely shear the top right off the sleigh.

"Did I ever tell you about Rule 49?" Kris asked Elaana.

"No. What's Rule 49?"

"DUCK!"

They both got down as the sleigh zipped toward the tree. Kris waited for the crash and crunch of wood on wood, certain Eldwin's craftsmanship was about to meet its match. The front of the sleigh lifted slightly, then it rocked back and forth gently, like a ship on the ocean.

"What just happened?" Elaana asked.

"I'm not sure I want to know," Kris said.

"Are you two all right back there?" Donder called.

Kris and Elaana poked their heads up above the edge of the sleigh. They were expecting to see tree trunks, but instead stared eye-to-eye with tree tops.

"Ho-ho-ho!" Kris laughed when he looked down. "We're flying!"

A pie-eyed Elaana peeked up over the edge and looked down. She slid back into the belly of the sleigh with a dizzy moan.

The sleigh soared high into the air. Kris could see the great tree at the center of their village, and a split-second later they landed at its base.

"I believe this is where you needed to go," Blitzen said.

"Actually," Kris said sheepishly, "I could stand to go a *bit* farther, if you are able."

Elaana elbowed him in his boney ribs. "Don't press your luck."

"Don't worry, m'lady. We're not tired at all. To be honest, I'm not even warmed up yet. How about you, team, are you too tired to go on?" Donder asked. All the other reindeer shook their heads.

"Then away we go!" Kris called, and they took off out of the Glen and into the night sky. The snow and ice passed quickly beneath them, a glowing white blur that soon gave way to the inky blackness of the nighttime sea.

"Look at that. It looks like a bunny," Elaana said, pointing to a cloud below them. The sleigh rocked gently on the currents of air as the reindeer pulled it toward Oldenton.

CHAPTER 19

A HELPING HAND

Aaron fell asleep in the branches of the tree, his arms wrapped loosely around the trunk. The wolves sat around the base licking their chops and looking up at him, waiting for him to lose his grip and fall.

Had Aaron been awake, he would have heard the miners on the road going home for the evening after a full day's work, but in his weakened and dreary state the sound did not catch his attention. Nor did the noise scare off the wolves. Aaron had missed his chance for help.

The wolves' ears perked up when a distant howl filtered through the woods, and they went off to investigate. Aaron's arms relaxed as he sank into a deeper sleep. His body leaned, then teetered, then fell from the branch. His eyes shot open and his hands reached for support but grabbed only air as he dropped to the ground.

Aaron landed on the carcass of the wolf he had stabbed, barely missing the handle of his knife. The fall knocked the breath out of him. Aaron tried to sit up, to breathe, but he could do neither. His leg throbbed, the pain intensifying with each heartbeat. He blinked his eyes and turned his head. A pair of red eyes stared at him from behind a distant tree. Then a howl pierced the air. From off in the woods, the echoes of the howl were met with responses.

Aaron's breath returned in hyperventilating gasps, and adrenaline coursed through his veins, giving him the energy to sit up and the awareness to extract his knife from the wolf beneath him. He reached for the tree branch above him to pull himself up but could not. Aaron tried to hobble to the road but fell the first time he put weight on his wounded leg, screaming in pain as he went down. The sound of the wolves drew nearer.

* * *

Alice heard someone on the street walking toward her house. It was probably John Constable making his nightly rounds. She took a deep breath to call out to him, but the slight movement was followed by a crack in the wood holding her up and her body dropped an inch as the weakened board came closer to breaking off completely. Her scream was reduced to a miserable little whimper and it failed to catch John Constable's attention; he walked on down the road, off to finish his patrol.

The moon climbed higher into the sky as the sun circled to the far side of the world, taking with it the last remnants of the day's heat. The chill air surrounded Alice, carving out goose-bumps on her tender young skin. The first time she shivered she wept, certain that the shaking would send her crashing to the ground, but it did not. She tried to will her body to stay still. Several minutes passed and she shivered again, stronger and longer this time. The trellis creaked and groaned.

* * *

Aaron stumbled onto the road, using a large stick as a cane. Crashing in the brush told him the pack of wolves was almost upon him. He readied his knife and held fast to the stick. Hope all but abandoned him as the first wolf appeared at the side of the road.

* * *

Alice could not fight her reflexes, and her body shivered hard against the cold night air, trying to generate heat. The creak of breaking boards was joined by the sound of ripping fabric and Alice found herself slowly inching toward the hard ground. *Someone help me, please!*

* * *

The sleigh came in high over the trees, the road snaking its way through the forest beneath them. Kris sat with his eyes closed, watching Aaron and Alice.

Kris' eyes snapped open. "Hurry, team, go faster if you can! We may be too late already," Kris called to the reindeer.

"There, right ahead!" Kris yelled. "Here, take the reins. Bring me in low, behind him," Kris told Elaana.

"What are you doing?" she asked as he climbed over the edge of the sleigh and stood on the long runner.

"You don't want to know," Kris said and ducked down out of sight.

Kris wrapped his legs around the runner and hung upside down, looking down the road at Aaron. He held his arms out and opened and closed his fingers, getting ready to make a grab.

* * *

The wolf walked to the middle of the road and turned to face Aaron. Its lips curled, exposing the sharp points of its teeth. The fur on its back stood on end and a low growl crept up from its throat. The wolf crouched and leapt at Aaron, its snarling jaws reaching for his throat.

Aaron swung the stick, striking the wolf in mid-air and knocking it to the ground. The wolf whimpered and growled as it moved to the back of the pack. Two other wolves moved in. Spittle sprayed from their lips as they snapped their jaws, edging closer, aware of the weapons in the hands of their prey.

Aaron heard a bark and at once the four wolves rushed him, the two in front leaping at him as their pack-mates stormed onto the road and attacked from both sides.

The sleigh swooped down as the wolves jumped at Aaron, and Kris grabbed the boy under his arms. Elaana pulled back on the reins and the reindeer took the sleigh up and over the trees, Kris and Aaron dangling under it. On the ground behind them, the four wolves collided in mid-air. They landed with a confused thump, letting out angry wails as their prize flew up and away.

"You must close your eyes, and promise me you will keep them closed," Kris said to Aaron.

"They are, I promise," Aaron said.

With one mighty swing Kris flipped Aaron up and into the sleigh, next to Elaana. Kris stood on the runner. "On to town, we mustn't delay."

* * *

Alice felt a warmth trickle down her back; the board holding her off the ground was also pressing into her back, and its persistence finally broke the skin. Her face glowed in the moonlight, looking like sweat but in all actuality it was dew drawn to her waning warmth. She had no energy left to cry. She dozed off and woke up, and when she opened her eyes and looked around at the stars high above and the ground far below she thought she was in a terrible dream, and she tried to wake herself.

She pinched her arm. It hurt, but the dream world was still there.

She closed her eyes. Darkness. She opened them and the dream returned, with its cold night air and dangerous heights.

She closed her eyes again, longer. *Wake up. Wake up. Wake up.*

She opened her eyes, and again the dream materialized before her. *Sometimes I can fly in my dreams.* She spread her arms like wings and arched her back.

Then she heard a loud crack, and in her dream she felt herself falling.

* * *

The sleigh sped through the town, inches from the rooftops. Cats and rats in alleyways scattered to the dark corners, and birds looked up from their nests at the blur that shook the trees.

The reindeers' legs pumped back and forth through the air, forcing the sleigh faster and faster still, reaching speeds that surprised even them. Elaana held the reins in a white-knuckled grip, and Aaron, eyes still closed, buried his head in her side.

Kris stood on the runner, looking forward, eyes squinting against the wind, which combed his white hair back and parted his beard in the middle, revealing a silvery depth that had lost all hints of its former redness.

"There!" Kris said, pointing to the house. "Go around to the far side."

The sleigh hopped over the roof and circled to the trellis. Kris looked at the spot where Alice had been. Elaana pulled back hard on the reins and the reindeer came to a halt on the roof as they looked down at the little girl lying prone on the ground.

Kris stepped off the runner and hurried across the sloped roof to the trellis. He stepped over the edge and floated to the ground. Kris knelt next to Alice. He checked her neck and wrist for a pulse.

"How is she?" Elaana called.

"Who?" Aaron asked. "Where are we?"

"Shhh," Elaana said. "We'll explain in a moment."

"She's unconscious, but alive," Kris called. "There's a bump on the back of her head, I swear it's as big as a Faerie's butt. And it looks like her arm is broken. I'm afraid to think of what illness the long exposure to the cold has brought on. We must get her inside."

Kris rose to the rooftop and then descended through the chimney. Once inside the house, he crossed the room to the front door and unlocked it, then he went around to the side of the house and carefully scooped Alice up and carried her inside.

Elaana held Aaron's hands and with a gentle leap they went from the roof to the ground. Once inside, Elaana put a blindfold on Aaron.

"Why can't I see you?" he asked.

"Rule 78," Kris said.

"What's Rule 78?"

"It says you aren't allowed to see us. Just trust us, it's important. We didn't make that Rule, but we do have to follow it."

"Where are we?"

"Your home."

"Is it Alice that's hurt?"

Aaron moved to tear the blindfold from his head but Elaana stayed his hand. "Yes," she said.

"Can you help her?"

"We'll try," Kris said. Alice lay on a fur rug before him. "Elaana, I need you to get two pieces of wood for a splint, and something to bind it."

"The wood pile is out back," Aaron said. "We're really low on kindling, but you should be able to find something you can use."

Kris held Alice's arm steady while Elaana fetched the wood.

"Once I get your sister's arm taken care of we'll get your leg cleaned up. I'm hoping that it looks worse than it really is," Kris said to Aaron.

"It really hurts."

"It'll get better."

"Will Alice be okay?"

"Her arm will be fine. It will take some time to heal, though. She's breathing steady and her heart is beating strong. We just need her to wake up so we know her head isn't hurt too bad."

"I'll do whatever I can to make her better."

"I know you will. So will I."

"Who are you?"

"I'm..." Kris stopped. He was certain these were his relatives, as certain as he was of his own name. But even so, he could not reveal himself to them. Rule 956: *Kris Kringle must remain anonymous.* It was for the safety of the Glen, and every Elf in it.

"Are you the man Alice calls Cinder Clouds?"

"Yes."

"You know, all the kids in Oldenton are talking about you. They say you're going to bring presents on Christmas Day."

"That's my plan."

Elaana came in with two small sticks and a short piece of rope. "This is all I could find."

"It will have to do," Kris said and set about securing the splint to Alice's arm, which he then set in a sling.

Elaana went back out and gathered up more kindling and logs to start a fire in the stove. "This wood doesn't burn easily," she said after the kindling burnt out, sending a nice plume of smoke up the chimney but failing to leave a fire burning in its wake.

"I know," Aaron said. "The seasoned wood has been picked over. I've been too busy at the mine to go deeper into the forest to find more. Now I'm not going to be able to do it because of my leg. I was going to bring a load of coal home with me today; our chute is empty, save some dust. Coal would get that wood burning quicker than the kindling."

Elaana grabbed two handfuls of coal dust from the chute. It was enough to start a fire in the stove. She put on a pot of water to boil and then walked over to Aaron.

"I'm going to check out your leg," she said.

Aaron winced as Elaana untied the shirt sleeve and rolled up his pants leg, which was stiff with dried blood. Dirt and grime clung to the thin hairs on his shin, but it did not cover up the puncture wounds from the wolf's fangs. Deep red craters perforated his calf.

Kris finished up with Alice and laid her on the couch as Elaana began to clean Aaron's leg. He sat in one chair while she propped his foot up on another. She set a pan under his leg and filled a pitcher with warm water from the stove. Aaron yelped as the water flowed over his wounds.

"Take off your belt," Kris said. Aaron did so and held the leather belt out to him. "I don't need it, you do. Fold it over and bite down on it."

Elaana wet a cloth and carefully wiped Aaron's leg clean. The salty taste of leather coated Aaron's mouth. The water in the pan under his leg grew dark.

"We need to make sure it doesn't get infected," Elaana said. "I can take the sleigh and find herbs to make a salve."

"Good idea. I'll stay here with the kids," Kris said. He sat down next to Alice and cradled her head in his lap.

* * *

When Elaana returned she found everyone asleep. She nudged Kris. "Must feel good to sleep with other humans for once."

Kris grinned and rubbed his eyes. "Best nap I've ever had."

They made the salve and applied the ointment to Aaron's leg before checking Alice again. When Elaana touched the knot on her head, Alice moaned and her eyelids danced as if to open but stayed shut.

"Alice, can you hear me?" Kris asked.

A soft mumble came from her mouth.

"You're going to be all right," Kris said. "You were hurt. You are home now, and we're taking care of you."

Alice's lips parted and closed, but she made no sound. Kris dipped his fingers in a cup of clean water and wet her lips. She licked at them. He did it again.

Once both children were tended to and put to bed, Elaana and Kris sat side by side on the couch, watching as the morning light crept in through the window. Outside, a cock crowed. Kris sat up straight.

"It's morning," he said.

"Yeah." Elaana stretched her arms wide. "What a night."

"You don't understand. People will be waking up, and we have a sleigh and eight reindeer parked on the roof!"

"Do you think anyone will notice?"

"Of course! Everyone will notice!"

"What do we do? We can't leave the kids."

"You take the sleigh. Come back for me tonight. I'll stay here," Kris stood up and walked to the front window. The streets were still cloaked in shadow, but the rooftops glowed with the first rays of morning light. He pulled the curtains closed. "Hurry. Go up through the chimney. Make sure you aren't seen!"

Elaana wasted no time. A scraping sound reverberated through the house as the sleigh took off. Kris made sure the doors and windows were locked and the curtains drawn. He slumped down on the couch in the darkened room, and within seconds he was sound asleep.

CHAPTER 20
AN IMPOSSIBLE TASK

Kris awoke to the clicks and clangs of a key in the front door lock. He bolted from the couch and disappeared up the chimney as Thomas opened the door and stepped inside. Kris squinted at the mid-day sun and did his best to stay hidden from view, ducking behind the chimney. He closed his eyes and reached inside the house with his mind.

Thomas looked around. He could tell something was awry. He walked over to the stove and held his hand over its surface. Warm. He opened the belly of the stove and blew on the black and gray coals. They flared orange and a small flame jumped up, danced for a moment, then faded away.

"Thomas," Kris called down the chimney.

Thomas closed the stove door and stood up. "Who's there?" he called.

"Over here."

Thomas walked toward the fireplace.

"Whcrc are you?"

"What are you doing here, Thomas?"

"How do you know my name?"

"I know a lot of things about you. More than you would like, probably. I've seen the things you've done. I know what you are about to do."

"And what's that?" Thomas asked.

"You need to leave them alone. They are hurt, and sick, and it's all because of you and your father. Their firewood is fresh and wet and they are almost out of kindling. It will be all they can do just to stay warm."

"They're trespassing. My father said they have to go, and it is my job to evict them. I know better than to disobey my father."

"Two days before Christmas, and you kick them out on the street? You can't!" Kris pleaded. He saw his hopes of proving human virtue fading with each word young Thomas spoke.

"No, you're right. I won't kick them out two days before Christmas," Thomas said.

Kris breathed a sigh of relief. *Perhaps Thomas isn't that bad, after all.*

"I'll do it Christmas Day," Thomas said. A noise came from the back bedroom and he turned toward it. "Oh, good. You're up."

Alice walked into the room, her splinted arm hanging in a sling. "What will you do on Christmas Day?"

"Kick you out of this house. Again."

Alice furrowed her brow and looked at him. Her memory was foggy. She remembered a dream where she was falling, but nothing from the prior day that led up to it.

"Will I still get my presents?" she asked.

"What presents? From Cinder Clouds?"

"Yes," Alice said. "I set out an evergreen branch, and he will bring me presents. He told me that anyone who leaves the branch out on Christmas Eve will have a present next to it on Christmas morning."

"You can use your evergreen branch to build a roof over your head, because you'll need one." Thomas took a step closer. "Cinder Clouds is a figment of your imagination."

"Then I'm a figment of your imagination, too. Who do you think you've been talking to?" Kris said. Thomas spun toward the chimney.

"*You're* Cinder Clouds? You mean you're real?" Thomas asked.

"Who ever said I wasn't?"

"No one, I guess. But Alice makes stuff up all the time. You can't trust her."

"It looks like you're wrong there."

"It doesn't matter. She can't stay here. Neither can her brother. I'm being generous by letting them stay until Christmas. They shouldn't even be here now. And neither should you!"

Thomas ran to the front door.

"Alice, close your eyes," Kris said.

"Why?"

"Just do it. Please!" Kris said and hopped into the chimney just as Thomas appeared in the street.

Kris popped out of the fireplace. Alice held her eyes shut tight. Kris spotted the key ring on the table, then ran to the front door and locked it. He heard Aaron's footsteps on the stairs and hid.

Thomas stared at the vacant roof for a minute before trying to get back inside. When the doorknob didn't turn he reached into his pocket for his keys. His hands coming up empty, Thomas pounded on the door with both fists and shouted for Alice to let him in. He punched the door, the coarse wood scraping skin from his knuckles. Thomas swore and started kicking the door.

The peephole opened. Aaron's face appeared on the other side. "Just go," he said.

Thomas scowled and turned to leave.

"And Thomas," Aaron said.

Thomas turned back to the door.

"Merry Christmas."

* * *

When Elaana returned that evening she found Kris sitting with Alice on his lap.

"I need to get you back to the Great Northern Glen," Elaana said.

Kris cradled Alice's head against his chest and brushed back a strand of hair that was stuck to her cheek. Alice coughed once, then harder a second time. She took a deep breath in, and a sound like water being sucked down a drain gurgled from her chest. She coughed again. Kris wiped the sputum off the side of her mouth with a towel.

"I can't leave. She's delirious with fever. She can hardly breathe. Aaron's leg is swollen and looks infected. If I go, who will take care of them?"

"Kris, you can't stay any longer. There's too much at risk."

"Their lives are at risk!"

"And so are the lives of every Elf in the Glen! You signed us up for a mission—"

"I didn't sign any Elf up. They all volunteered."

"Right. Every Elf volunteered. They sacrificed their futures for you. Their families. They are working like mad to make the toys you had on your list. You can't just cancel Christmas, not now. Plus, you promised all the other kids in this town, not just Aaron and Alice. You have to make good on that promise."

"It's hopeless. We couldn't even make two quick stops in time. There's no way I'll be able to deliver a present to every child in town in one night. What was I thinking?"

"You were thinking about your family. You were going to prove to my father what you know about human virtue."

"Ahh, yes. Humans have no virtue. Look at Horace, look at Thomas. Do they have virtue? It's a farce."

"No it's not."

"Look at this little girl. She's sick, and she may die. She needs warmth. The logs are wet. The kindling has run out, and they are in no condition to go out and get more. If this fire goes out, they'll never get another one lit. And do you know why she's like this? Because her Uncle Horace is mad at his step-father, a man who has been dead for twenty years. And her cousin Thomas is just a young boy who refuses to think for himself. He's shouldered his father's hatred as if it were his own. How can a parent soil a child like that? How can I prove virtue in the face of such indignities?"

"You will."

"How?"

"I don't know. I never knew. I just trusted you. You said the Great Northern Glen would be there, and it was. We thought we wouldn't be able to pull the sleigh, and now we have a team of flying reindeer! Kris, things just have a way of working out for you. You need to trust yourself."

Elaana walked behind the couch and leaned over him, putting her arms around him. She kissed him on the cheek. "If we work together, quickly, we can find some medicine to take the edge off her cough."

"Bringing medicine is against the Rules. I'd bring them firewood, but I can only bring what they asked for, and only on Christmas Day."

"Nonsense. Healing the sick breaks no Rule. Ask your mother. I'll take that one up with my father any day. And once we give Alice medicine, there are plenty of blankets and furs here to bundle her up, and there's food and water..."

"She can't feed herself. Even if she could, she can't keep anything down. I won't let her die."

"It is not your fate to determine hers. You've done all you can. Now you have to get back on your own path. Aaron will look after her. She's a strong little girl. She's fighting this. And when she wakes up on Christmas morning, she damn well better see the doll house you promised her!"

Kris looked at Alice's face, her cheeks flushed with fever, her forehead clammy with sweat. He glanced over at the fireplace. The evergreen branch lay beside it, placed there the very night Kris first visited Alice.

"You're right," he said. "I did make a promise. And I'm a man of my word."

Kris laid Alice down on the couch and fixed pillows and blankets to keep her warm. He set a bucket near her head in case she got sick. He pulled a small table close and set a clean towel on it, and next to the towel he placed some water and bread.

Elaana checked on Aaron and changed the bandage on his leg. He woke up in the process, but Elaana was able to see well enough to work in a dark room so he could not see her.

"Thank you," he whispered.

"You're welcome," she said. "Sleep now, and heal. You and your sister will be all right."

Kris and Elaana disappeared up the chimney and took off in the sleigh. They flew south, to a place where it was still warm enough for mint and other herbs to thrive, and on the way back to the house Elaana made a soothing rub for Alice's chest to help her breathe, and an ointment to fight the infection in Aaron's leg.

When at last Kris was satisfied that they had done all they could for the children, they took off for the Great Northern Glen.

CHAPTER 21
FLY HOME, BLACKBIRD

Jason watched his father read, something he missed dearly. Growing up, he always got a story before bed. Nowadays he got lectures all day and nothing at night.

He looked around the room. Everyone was staring at his dad. Jason bet they all missed the stories they got growing up too.

The radio crackled when Professor Hodgin paused to take a sip of water. Dan's voice chopped through the static.

"Professor, I have to bring it in. I'm low on fuel. Any more of this and we won't make it back to the ship."

Professor Hodgin clicked the button on the microphone. "Roger that. Fly home, Blackbird."

"We should go out by snowmobile," Juan said. "I'll climb down the crevice."

"I won't risk it. You could be killed," Professor Hodgin said.

"I'll sign a waiver first. I promise I won't sue. Seriously. Tie the end of a rope to a snowmobile and lower me in. Then you can pull me out really fast."

"And if the rope breaks?" Professor Nara asked.

"We'll use two ropes," Juan said, "one for backup."

"If you just go down ten feet to get a better view..." Professor Hodgin said and rubbed the stubble on his chin. "There might be more books, or other artifacts down there."

"I bet there's enough for a traveling show, like the King Tut or Titanic exhibits. But since this is Santa's stuff, we'll get to tour every year. Think about what we can do with that money," Juan said. "Talk about commercializing Christmas!"

"You're forgetting something," Jason said.

"What?"

"Santa's still alive, and this book is probably his. It's not ours to sell."

"Finders keepers," Juan said.

Jason crossed his arms. "Grow up."

"Hold on now," Professor Hodgin said. "Jason, this book may be the greatest archeological discovery of our lifetime. It's important in so many ways...you're just too young to see it."

"Too young? I'm old enough to see that Juan is the one who's acting like a baby. You all think this book is so important, and you're reading the words, but you don't understand what the book is saying, do you? I mean, I'm just a kid and I get it."

"What should we do then, big man?" Juan asked.

"Finish reading it," Jason said. "After that, I'll tell you *my* master plan."

CHAPTER 22
ONE MORE CHRISTMAS WISH

Kris and Elaana rode the sleigh north. They were barely out of town when Kris closed his eyes for a moment. "We have to turn back," he said when he opened them.

"What? Are you crazy? Kris, there isn't the time. I told you Alice will get better." Elaana said.

"It's not Alice. It's Thomas. You won't believe what he's doing."

* * *

Thomas held the evergreen branch behind his back as he crossed the kitchen. His mother was bent over the chopping block cutting up a chicken and didn't notice him. Thomas walked into the empty parlor and knelt in front of the fire.

"What are you doing with that?" his father asked, standing at the doorway behind Thomas. Thomas whirled around. "Take it outside. It's just going to smoke and pop. Evergreen's no good for a fire. Especially inside."

Thomas stared at the branch. His hand quivered. "I was just—"

"I said take it outside."

"But I—"

Horace took a step toward Thomas and Thomas ran out the door. Outside, he shivered looked up at the moon high in the sky. Something passed in front of it in a dark blur and was gone; it looked like the negative image of a shooting star, a dark shape forming suddenly out of the void of night and racing back into non-existence.

As much as Alice liked to play pretend-games, Thomas could no longer doubt Cinder Clouds was real, not after hearing his voice. Every child in Oldenton talked about the gifts they asked for. Thomas didn't want to be the only one who didn't get a special present on Christmas morning. He had to find a way to get the branch out by the fireplace on Christmas Eve.

Thomas walked over to the coal bin next to the wood pile and sat down on its heavy lid and rubbed his arms for warmth. His mind struggled in vain to think up reasons to bring the evergreen branch back inside. Behind the wood pile, a twig snapped. Thomas sat up straight.

"Don't be alarmed. It's me, Cinder Clouds. We never got the chance to finish our conversation."

"You have to leave! If my father sees you—"

"I'm not afraid of your father. I need you to tell me what you want for Christmas. But I must give you warning: You have been a very naughty boy. I don't have to bring you anything."

"Will you, though?"

"That depends."

"On what?"

"On you. Tell me now, what do you want me to bring you for Christmas?"

"I want a sword and a helmet. One day I want to be a knight."

"Really, a knight? Are you sure you're cut out for it? Tell me what you know about knights."

"They fight, and protect the kingdom, and they're rich, and the maidens swoon for them. My dad said knights enforce the law of the land. That people have to do what they say."

"And then what did your dad tell you?" Kris asked.

Thomas lowered his head. "To kick Alice and Aaron out of their house."

"Is that why you want to be a knight? So you can spend your days forcing people out into the cold, hurting them? Alice almost died because of what your dad made you do. Did you know that?"

Thomas shook his head. "No," he said softly.

"I know a lot about knights," Kris said, "more than your father. Knights are quite virtuous. They have to be selfless, caring naught for themselves and giving their life in the service of others. They do fight, but they have the risk of returning with no reward, save battle scars...if they return at all. Can you do that? Can you give and ask nothing in return?"

Thomas was silent. He had never thought of knighthood that way before. "I think so."

"Then maybe I'll bring you bring you a present."

"So what are you getting for Christmas?"

"Who, me?" Kris asked.

"Yeah, you. Don't tell me you go through all this work to bring kids presents and then don't get any gifts yourself."

"Actually, that's exactly how it works."

"That's dumb."

"Thomas, there's more to it than presents. Think of me as a knight. I give, and I ask nothing in return."

"So you'll bring me something?"

No answer.

"Please? It doesn't have to be a sword and helmet. Just bring me *something*!"

Thomas got up and raced around the wood pile. Vacant. He looked toward the woods. Around the edge of the path a few leaves swayed as if pushed by a breeze, but the night was still, there was no wind.

"Cinder Clouds?"

Above him the dark streak returned, lower and larger this time but no less swift; as quickly as it appeared it was gone.

* * *

The sleigh descended through the entrance to the Great Northern Glen without touching a single flake of snow. It circled the top of the great tree while Kris called out to the Elfs gathering below.

"Christmas Eve is upon us! Are we ready to go?"

Every manner of no floated up through the trees as the Elfs begged for more time.

"Ho-ho-ho!" Kris laughed. "Fear not. You'll be done on time, or I'm a fat-bottomed Faerie! Tomorrow will be a special day, for us, and for the children of Oldenton. The work you do today will never be forgotten."

The sleigh landed and came to a stop in front of the toy factory. Kris opened the doors wide and stared in at the commotion. Through clouds of sawdust he saw Elfs bent over tables, piecing together carved wood, sewing clothes for a variety of dolls (it turns out Alice's request was not uncommon), testing the bounciness of balls and the crack of bats as all the toys were finished. Eldwin wrapped the presents, double-checking each label to make sure no child would receive the wrong gift.

"We need to help," Kris said to Elaana.

"No, they're fine," Elaana said, closing the door. "You need to eat. I'm going to turn you into a fat-bottomed Faerie to keep you warm. But that will take time, and since we don't have the time right now, you need to come with me."

Kris followed Elaana to his cabin. Elaana pointed to the back bedroom. "Go in there, look in your closet. I'll wait out here."

Kris disappeared into the bedroom and closed the door.

"Ho-ho-ho! I like it!"

"Put it on and see if it fits."

"I got my red back!" Kris jumped into the parlor. He wore matching pants and coat made of red fur, laced with edges as white as his beard and hair. His new suit swayed on his thin frame as he danced a happy jig. "It's a big large, though."

"That's why I needed you to try it on. I can take it in a little bit, but once I get some insulation under your skin it'll fit snug."

Elaana knelt next to Kris. She pulled a pencil from her pocket and marked the bright red coat as she folded it so it fit tighter. Then she ordered Kris back into the bedroom to change again so she could make alterations.

"This is why I hate getting new clothes," Kris called from the bedroom. "All this dressing and undressing and dressing again. Who needs it?"

"You do. And you better be polite, this is your Christmas present from the Elfs. Even if it was just socks and underwear, you should be thankful someone thought enough to give you something," Elaana said as Kris handed her the suit.

"I like the suit. It's just all the—"

"Hush."

"Right."

Kris ate a loaf of bread and bowl of soup while Elaana hemmed his coat and pants. She even fitted him with a matching hat.

"Now you really have your red back," she said as she reached up and pulled the hat over his curly white hair.

Kris admired himself in the mirror. Elaana stood next to him and put her arms around his waist. "Are you warm?" she asked.

"Next to you, always."

CHAPTER 23

FIRE AND ICE

A small flame jumped to and fro in the fireplace while Aaron slept on the couch. The morning sun had not yet reached the window, and when the flame had had its fill of fun it leapt out of sight and darkness overtook the room.

The shift from dull light to inky black reached Aaron's sleeping mind and he opened his eyes in a panic. He swung his feet off the couch and stood up, then yelped in pain as he fell upon his wounded leg. He crawled to the fireplace and grabbed the poker, blowing on the logs as he moved them, trying to bring the flame back to life. A lone cinder rose into the chimney.

Aaron gave up on the fire and returned to the couch. When dawn finally broke it did so without any fanfare, the warm rays of the sun unable to penetrate the dense winter clouds that were ready to burst with snow. The air in the house moved as a strong wind forced itself through the cracks around the windows and eaves. The temperature in the room dropped several degrees.

Aaron dozed lightly for an hour. Alice's moaning tickled his ears and drew him from his slumber. He hobbled into the bedroom to check on his sister.

The room was dark, and without fire to light a candle he had to pull back the curtains to see. Cool winter air snuck in and Aaron shivered. He eased himself onto the side of the bed and put his palm on Alice's forehead. His mother always did that. When he was little Aaron tried to feel the temperature on Alice's forehead himself, but it never felt hot. This time, Alice's forehead could fry an egg. Her fever had risen during the night.

Alice's eyelids fluttered. "Thank you Mommy," she mumbled. Aaron kissed her forehead, just like their mother used to do. She gave a weak smile and closed her eyes. He took the towel that lay on the table beside her bed and wiped the sweat from her face. A tear fell from his cheek and landed on hers. He wiped that away, too.

Aaron re-arranged the sheets and pillow so the spots dripping wet from her sweat were on the other side of the bed. She wheezed and coughed whenever he moved her. The sounds of the fluid filling her lungs grew more distinct. He had never been more afraid in his whole life, not even when facing down a pack of wolves. He lost his parents. He lost the mine. Now he stood to lose his little sister as well.

Aaron pulled the curtains shut to preserve what warmth the room still held and hobbled back into the parlor. The house creaked and moaned under the force of the wind outside. Aaron wrapped himself in a fur and sat on the couch. Something told him that the worst was yet to come.

* * *

Thomas sat on his bedroom floor and searched through the bottom drawer of his dresser.

"I thought I told you to fill the coal bin," Horace said to Thomas from the doorway. Horace had come home with a large wagon full of coal, too much to dump directly into the bin like he normally did so he had dumped the coal in the shed.

"Yes sir, you did," Thomas said.

"Then why is the bin empty? Do you need a reminder of what happens when you don't listen?" Horace cracked his knuckles.

"No sir. I'll getting ready to do it right now. I'm sorry."

Thomas found the old stockings he was looking for and pulled them on. He had to yank hard, they barely fit his feet anymore. The little toe on his right foot poked through a hole and stared up at him like an ugly little worm. He let his pants leg drop, covering up the patterns that were woven into the stockings.

Thomas bundled up and went outside. The wind grabbed his hat from his head and tried to carry it off, but Thomas was able to catch it. He pulled it back down over his ears, which stung from the brief exposure.

The snow had already started to accumulate and Thomas left tracks as he made his way across the yard to the shed. Once inside he filled two buckets and clipped thin chains to their handles. The chains were attached to a long board. He shouldered the board and stood straight. The buckets lifted off the ground and swung on either side of him so he looked like a merchant's scale.

Thomas carried the coal to the bin beside the kitchen door. The bin extended into the house and had another door inside the kitchen, so they would not have to go outside for coal when the bin was full. He lifted the bin's heavy outer lid and dumped in the contents of each bucket. It didn't even cover a quarter of the bottom of the bin, let alone fill it to the top, two—feet deep. He shouldered the board again and made his way back to the shed.

After a dozen trips he looked in the bin. Only halfway done.

I bet knights never have to slog coal across the yard. They have squires and knaves to do it for them.

On the eighteenth round the chains holding one basket broke, and Thomas had to carry the heavy buckets by hand.

"Stupid dirty black rocks," Thomas said to himself as he struggled with the final load.

Thomas didn't see the edge of the flagstone path and stepped off it. The odd shift in balance sent the buckets swaying, and Thomas with it. He tried to steady himself but his feet gave way on the snowy ground and he and the coal went spilling.

Snow puffed up as Thomas pounded the ground and yelled in frustration. He climbed to his knees and looked around. Black streaks in the fresh snow radiated out from each bucket, paths of dust leading to each rock sitting half-buried in the snow.

"I hate you," Thomas said to each lump of coal as he filled the buckets. "And I hate *you*...And I hate *you*..."

When he finally finished he went inside. He took off his boots by the door and hung up his hat and coat, then he went into the parlor and sat down in front of the fireplace and peeled off his stockings.

"You still have those? I can't believe it. You got those stockings when you were ten. Look at them, they don't even hold all your toes in," his mother said.

"Yeah, they're comfortable though," Thomas said and laid them next to the fireplace.

"What are you doing?" his mother asked.

"They're wet. I'm just drying them."

"Oh, don't bother. Throw them out. Look at them, they're rags."

"What happened to 'waste not, want not'?"

"These are different times. We don't need to go around looking like peasants. Give those here, I'll put them in the trash."

"Wait...shouldn't we let them dry first? Otherwise they'll just stink up the bin."

"Oh, I suppose. Hang them on the mantle. They'll dry better that way."

Thomas hung the stockings from small pegs that ran along the front of the mantle. The forest of evergreen trees woven into the fabric waved like a flag in the breeze as the warm air drafted up from the fireplace. He didn't know if it would pass Cinder Clouds' rules, but it was the only shot he had.

He sat on the couch and waited, hoping Cinder Clouds would bring him a present.

* * *

Back at the North Pole, Kris enjoyed a second serving of a hearty stew and bread while Elaana helped Eldwin finish wrapping the presents. He had to admit, having a full belly did make him feel warmer.

"If Elaana's goal is to fatten me up, she'll have met it by the next full moon on this diet," he said to himself. He stood and stretched, then put on his hat and coat and walked out to the sleigh.

The reindeer were gathered around a water trough. "These feed bags the Elfs prepared are wonderful," Blitzen said. "Much better than having to dig nuts out of pine cones ourselves."

"Yes," Donder agreed. "And it's nice to finally have some new company."

"What's wrong with us?" Dancer asked.

"Nothing at all..."

"Ho-ho-ho! Just because you gain new friends doesn't mean you lose your family," Kris said. "We're all glad to be together, present company most definitely included." Kris scratched Dancer behind her ears.

"Are you ready for tonight?" Donder asked Kris.

"Almost. We still need to load up the sleigh. And I'm sure Elaana will try to feed me once more, but I'm afraid that if she does I'll be too heavy for you to pull."

"Nonsense. You'll never have a load too large for us," Comet said.

"We'll see. If we can pull tonight off, I'm going to try to bring presents to children all over the world next year!"

Prancer coughed and kicked Comet. "You had to open your mouth..."

* * *

Kris walked over to the toy factory. Elaana tied a bow on a present and set it at the base of a stack of boxes twice the size of the sleigh.

Kris let out a low whistle. "Is this everything?"

"All except one..." Eldwin said.

"Don't worry, I have that one covered." Kris walked around the pile. "There's a lot more kids in Oldenton than I thought. Funny, the list didn't look that long. So any clues as to how we are going to fit all this in the sleigh? I can't make more than one trip. Do we have a trailer or something?"

"I've got something better," Eldwin said. "Look here."

Eldwin reached into his pocket and pulled out a small square of red fabric with gold trim around the edges. "We can put it all in this."

"Have you been drinking Faerie dew? There's no way all of these presents will fit in that hanky."

"Says who?" Eldwin snapped the hanky and it popped open, and suddenly he held a sack large enough to climb into. The gold trim ringed the opening at the top.

"Impressive, but still..."

Eldwin let go of the sack and it fell to the ground in a large red pile. He reached into it with both hands and pulled out a large dollhouse. The gold trim snagged on the corner of the porch, keeping the sack open for a moment. Kris peeked inside. He saw nothing, just red fabric.

Eldwin set the dollhouse down, then turned his hands back to the sack. He rummaged around for a bit and pulled out a rocking horse. "Give me a hand with this, will you?"

"Glad to," Kris said, taking a hold of the horse's head. "Anything else in there I should know about?"

"That's it for now. But we need to fill it back up."

"How does it work?" Kris asked.

"It's a special kind of fabric, it's woven with Faerie dust. There are pockets in here, more pockets than you'll ever need." Eldwin held the bag open and let Kris look inside. Thousands of tiny pockets lined the sides like a lush red honeycomb.

"The pocket stretches when you open it." Eldwin set the bag on the ground and pulled out a pocket. It was so tiny he had to pinch it with his fingers, but it expanded easily and in a second Eldwin was standing up holding a sheet. "Once you close the pocket around something, the pocket goes back to its original size, no matter the size of the item you just put in it."

Eldwin wrapped the sheet over the toy horse. He rocked the horse back and forth to get the sheet under its feet. Once the horse was covered entirely, Eldwin let the sheet go and it snapped back inside the sack, with the horse inside it. The sack fluttered but quickly settled back to its original size.

"How did you get it in your pocket?" Kris asked.

"You fold it inside out. Watch." He held the gold trim up in front of him and curled it slightly outward. The sack hung a foot off the ground. Eldwin lifted the sack straight up and then snapped it straight down. The gold trim went over the bottom of the sack, then with one hand Eldwin snapped the trim sideways. He handed the hanky to Kris.

Kris stared at the small square of cloth draped over his hand.

"You'll get used to it," Eldwin said. "Practice by loading a few things into it. It's almost time for you to leave."

* * *

Aaron shivered. He watched his sister's breath puff up from her mouth in feeble little clouds. The cold air teased him by illustrating how shallow her breaths were. Her fever raged like an angry inferno, a cruel contrast to the frigid air that filled the room.

Aaron went to his parents' bedroom upstairs. He pulled a fine linen robe from his mother's closet. He held it to his face and breathed deep. The smell of her perfume tickled his nose and for a moment he was back in her arms.

Alice's coughing downstairs brought him back to reality and Aaron carried the robe to the fireplace. He tore at the cuff of a sleeve until he had a ball of string big enough to fill both his hands. He put the string in the fireplace and took a knife and block of flint and struck the knife furiously against the flint. A shower of sparks rained down on the string. Most fizzled in the air. A few fizzled on the fabric. One stuck to a string and burned.

Aaron cupped his hands around the string and watched it burn in two directions. The flame crossed paths against two other strings, and they too caught fire. Aaron blew gently and the fire spread farther, its heat radiating to the edge of the fireplace. Aaron moved the logs closer. They didn't catch. The string burned away too fast.

Aaron took the robe and shredded it and placed it in a great heap in the fireplace. He would get a fire started. He would keep his sister warm.

Aaron slashed at the flint with the knife. Sparks flared for their short lives. Aaron grunted as he made more. The fire teased him, jumping from string to string but not catching.

"Come on."

Aaron slowed down and struck the flint harder. Bigger sparks flew. He took a breath, hoisted the knife high, and brought it down again full force. Several large sparks flew off at random angles, missing the cloth completely. Aaron lifted the flint to move it and found himself holding only half of it. The other piece clacked on the stone fireplace. He picked up the larger piece and struck at it with the knife, fast and furious. Sparks flooded the bottom of the fireplace. Fire bit into the cloth and ate away.

Aaron fed the flames, moving the logs closer so they could catch. The fresh wood smoked, reluctant to burn. He needed something that would burn hotter and longer. He looked around the room. The closest thing to him that was made of wood thin enough to break apart was his father's old chair at the end of the kitchen table. The half-dozen thin wooden spokes inside the frame of the chair's back would make for excellent kindling.

Aaron knocked the chair over and grabbed it by a leg. He lifted the chair and struck it against the floor. It creaked and splintered but did not break. He lifted the chair again, and as he hoisted it over his head the weight of the chair shifted and the leg in his hands twisted and came loose. The rest of the chair crashed to the ground.

Aaron scooted over to the fireplace and tossed the chair leg into the fire. It landed with its top facing out and Aaron noticed a plug of cork in it. He pulled the leg back out of the fire and set it aside, curious. Orange embers traced patterns in the wood where it had started to burn. He limped back to the chair and smashed it against the floor again, succeeding in breaking the back frame and loosening the spokes. He gathered them up and tossed them into the fire.

The kindling from the chair did burn, and as it did it heated up the larger logs. The heat from the fire was not enough to fight against the draft of cold air spilling down the chimney, though, and the smoke from the wet wood billowed into the parlor. Aaron coughed and blew on the fire to make it burn hotter. His efforts produced a larger plume of smoke that surrounded him and flooded the room behind him.

The wind outside howled, laughing at his feeble efforts to combat its escalating cold. The draft pushed down through the chimney, refusing to allow even a wisp of smoke upward.

Aaron turned around when he heard Alice coughing. He hobbled through the haze and into the back bedroom, unable to get ahead of the thick cloud of smoke. Alice tried to sit up to catch her breath, the miasma settling over her bed and denying her the fresh air for which she fought.

"Oh, Alice, I'm so sorry!" Aaron closed the bedroom door and opened the window. Cold air whipped through the room. Aaron's teeth chattered; he could only imagine the effect the smoke and the cold had on his sick little sister. He closed the window amid Alice's new fit of coughing and went back to the parlor, shutting the bedroom door firmly behind him. He had to put the fire out.

Aaron stood the logs up at the back of the fireplace, moving them as far from the kindling as he could to stop the slow burn that made so much smoke. He scattered the kindling so the fire would die out.

Aaron lined the bottom of Alice's door with blankets, then opened the front door to air the house out. The temperature plummeted, but the fresh air diluted the smoke. Aaron closed the door and went back to the bedroom.

"It hurts when I breathe," Alice said.

"I know. I'm sorry. The smoke's stopped now."

"I'm cold."

Aaron put another blanket over her. "The fire went out. I can't get a new one lit." He handed Alice a cup of water. "Drink this."

She took a sip and settled back onto her pillow. Aaron sat on the edge of the bed next to her and rubbed his hands together to warm them. The sun hadn't even gone down yet.

CHAPTER 24
GIFTS, EXPECTED AND UNEXPECTED

When all the presents were in the bag it wouldn't fold up to hanky-size anymore, but it looked empty. Kris climbed aboard the sleigh.

"Donder, is the team ready?" Kris asked.

"Always," Donder answered.

Elaana and Eldwin stood in front of a crowd of Elfs. Kris waved to them all and gave the reins a snap. The reindeer sped through the Glen and up the crevice, taking to the air as they reached its mouth. Kris relished the warmth of his new red suit as he steered the team south, toward Oldenton.

* * *

After the sun went down, the chill of night entered the room as if invited, but it most certainly was not. Aaron sat on the couch with Alice in his lap. At least her fever kept him warm.

* * *

Thomas snuck out of bed after his parents were asleep. He went into the parlor and sat in front of the fireplace, looking up at his stockings.

"Cinder Clouds," he whispered, "please bring me a present. It doesn't have to be a sword. I'm not ready to be a knight. But I will be one day. I'll prove it to you. I swear, I'll do whatever it takes. Just please, *please, pleeeease* bring me a present tonight. You choose. Whatever you want to bring me."

He sat and waited. *Cinder Clouds is real. He came here before. He'll come back.*

* * *

The reindeer landed on the rooftop, knocking snow to the ground. Kris climbed down from the sleigh and steadied himself against the wind as he walked across the crest of the roof to the chimney with his bag. He winked at the reindeer and disappeared to the fireplace below.

Kris walked into the room and stared at Aaron and Alice. *My family. A brother and sister I can laugh with and nap with. A family I could take care of. The family I've been searching for my whole life.*

Alice coughed and Kris snapped to, afraid he would be seen. He had come too far to start breaking the Rules. He ducked behind a chair.

A brother and sister I have to hide from.

They can't be my family. Not the way I want them to be.

Kris crept over to the couch. He placed his hand on Alice's forehead. Still hot. Alice adjusted herself and snuggled back against her big brother's chest.

Rest child, and heal, and when you wake up you'll have your present. Hopefully that will help you feel better.

Kris reached into his sack and pulled out the dollhouse—complete with a horse and carriage and clothes and everything else that was required.

For Aaron, Kris left a new pair of boots. He set them on the fireplace next to the burnt chair leg.

"Merry Christmas," he said, and was away, up the chimney.

* * *

Thomas forced his eyelids to stay open, fixated on the fireplace and the evergreen trees stitched into his stocking.

Please, Cinder Clouds. Please bring me a present. I can't be the only one without a gift tomorrow.

* * *

Kris went to the other kids' houses. Beside their evergreen branches he left toys, games, dresses, candy, and a dozen other answers to their wishes. He moved fast and silent, and the reindeer never tired. The wind and the snow tried to stop them, and although it slowed them down, they were determined to deliver all the presents. As dawn approached, the sack was emptied. But the night was not over yet. There was one house left.

They flew to Thomas' house.

Kris had kept an eye on Thomas all night. He heard every promise and every plea. He would leave Thomas a present. It would not be what the boy was expecting, and Kris hoped Thomas would figure out what to do with it.

Inside, Thomas finally lost his long battle with sleep. After several long blinks, each slightly longer than the one before it, his eyelids sealed shut and would stay that way until the rays of morning light teased them back open. He didn't see or hear a thing when Kris filled his stocking.

Kris folded the empty sack and put it in his pocket. He climbed into the sleigh and took off into the night, back to the Great Northern Glen. He landed on the ice up top and had the team walk the sleigh down the crevice and into the Glen. One of the Elfs spotted him coming through the trees and jingled a line of bells that hung next to the toy factory door. Elaana, Eldwin, and all the other Elfs came running to greet him.

"How did it go?" Elaana asked.

"Better than expected."

"Did you make that last stop?"

"I did."

"What did you give him?"

"I gave him the opportunity to redeem himself."

"Do you think he will?"

"I'm counting on it. We all should be. Believe it or not, Thomas is holding our ticket home."

Kris sat back, eyes closed, and watched as the scene unfolded in his mind. He spoke, narrating the events to Elaana, Eldwin, and all the other Elfs. They hung on every word, silent, hoping that Thomas would not find a way to blow it.

* * *

Frost lined the inside of the windows. Aaron sat up slowly, easing Alice off of his lap and missing her warmth when he stood. He noticed the fresh bandage on his leg, and then saw the dollhouse next to the fireplace. He looked at his sister, tempted to wake her. He decided to let her sleep. Her breath still rattled and her fever still burned.

Aaron worried that each breath of cold air was only making her worse. He knew she needed a fire. He needed a fire, or he would catch ill, too. He wanted to try to start one again, but he knew his mother's robe didn't burn hot enough. The wood from the chair was too thick to work as tinder. He needed something thinner like...the wood from the dollhouse.

"No, you can't," he said to himself.

But she'll never get the chance to play with it if you don't. She could die.

"No. Not yet."

* * *

Thomas opened his eyes. His father's snores rumbled down the hall from the back bedroom. He looked at his stockings. There was something inside one of them, weighing it down. Stretching it. Something heavy.

He grabbed the stocking off the hook and tip-toed back to his bedroom. He winced as the stocking banged against the frame of the door. His first instinct told him that the loud knock would wake his father. Then he worried that whatever Cinder Clouds had brought him might have broken.

Thomas closed the door and opened the curtains. The early morning light poured into the room. He sat on his bed and reached into the stocking. Whatever it was, it was very hard. It didn't feel broken. It had smooth sides, but its edges were sharp, and it was oddly shaped. It wasn't a box, it was just a lump.

He pulled it out and set it on the bed in front of him.

Cinder Clouds gave him a lump of coal. *Stupid coal.*

Thomas stared at the black rock. He had been so happy Cinder Clouds actually brought him a present; he hadn't considered that the present might be the one thing in the world he didn't want.

Who cares about dumb old coal. You should have brought coal to Aaron and Alice, they're the ones who need it.

He watched the snow swirl in the breeze. The storm had abated, but the air was no less frigid than the prior day. *I would hate to be without a fire on a day like today.*

Thomas remembered what Cinder Clouds said to him about knights. Could he give something up and ask for nothing in return? Well, actually, when that something was a stupid lump of coal he didn't even want to begin with, no problem!

Thomas got dressed. It was early. He could get there and back before breakfast.

This is easy! Knighthood, here I come...

* * *

Aaron sat on the hearth and reached for his new boots. He bumped the chair leg and it rolled onto the floor with a hollow thud. Alice opened her eyes a squint and looked toward the sound, and then opened them wide as saucers when she saw her present.

Alice sat up. "He came! I knew he would."

Aaron laced up his boots and stood up. He scooped up his sister and carried her to the fireplace. He kissed her cheek. The sweat that had dried to her face made his lips salty.

"Did Cinder Clouds bring you what you wanted?" Aaron asked.

Alice scrutinized the dollhouse. It was practically a palace. The horse and carriage could ride through the entry hall. Its dining room came complete with a table, twelve chairs, and a bureau of miniature plates and silverware. Tiny books lined the shelves of the library. Each of the seven bedrooms had a bed with a canopy, and under each canopy laid a doll. The closets were packed with clothes, and another doll dressed like a chef sat in the kitchen among a slew of pots and pans.

"I think so," she said as she held the prettiest doll up to the light. She set the doll back down in its bed and crawled over to the couch and curled up under the blankets.

"Don't you want to play with your new toy?" Aaron asked.

"It's too cold."

Aaron sat next to her. "At least my feet are warm." He held up his good leg and admired his new boot.

Alice fell back asleep. A light knock on the door startled Aaron. He hobbled over and opened the peephole, dreading the freezing air that would force its way in. The cold air froze Aaron's heart when it revealed Thomas's face on the other side.

"Merry Christmas," Thomas said.

"Here to kick us out?" Aaron asked.

"No. I have something for you."

"What?" Aaron asked, narrowing his eyes.

Thomas held a lump of coal up to the peephole. "Do you want this?"

Aaron closed the peephole. Thomas turned to go, but the door opened behind him.

"Come on in," Aaron said.

Thomas stepped inside with a bucket full of coal. Aaron closed the door. Thomas started to take off his coat, but realized that the air inside was barely warmer than the air outside and he put it back on. He walked over to the fireplace and set the bucket of coal in front of it. "Do you have any tinder?"

"I used threads from my mother's robe last night. I can get another," Aaron said.

"You're burning up your mother's clothes?" Thomas asked.

"What other choice do I have?" Aaron said and went upstairs. Thomas looked around. Alice was sound asleep on the couch. He spied the chair leg on the floor next to him and picked it up. He picked at the cork and it popped out. There was something inside the leg. Thomas pulled at it. Paper. A small piece tore off. He pulled again, carefully, and a large, rolled-up sheet emerged.

"Never mind," he called to Aaron. "I found something that will work."

Thomas unrolled the paper and read it.

The Last Will and Testament of Richard Miner.

It was dated that very year.

"This is the real will. My father's copy was from before Aaron was born," he whispered. He read through it quickly. He didn't need Count Whitley to tell him what the will said. It was obvious. The mine belonged to Aaron. So did the house, the horse, and many other things.

Thomas looked at the knife and flint. A quick stroke and a shower of sparks and the paper would go up in an instant. No one would know. His father would own the mine, and one day it would pass on to him. Thomas would have coal for the rest of his life.

"I think this one will work," Aaron called from the bedroom.

Burn it! Burn it quick! Thomas set the will in the fireplace. *Did Aaron even know this was in there?*

Thomas picked up the knife and angled the flint. He looked at the burn patterns on the chair leg.

No. He couldn't have known. Aaron was about to burn it himself. Now's the time. Burn it!

Aaron's footsteps sounded on the stairs.

No.

Thomas stood up and turned to face his cousin.

"You're the miner, not me," he said as Aaron reached the bottom step. Thomas crossed the room and handed Aaron the paper. "I'm going to be a knight."

"What is this?" Aaron asked.

"Read it. I found it in here." Thomas held up the hollow chair leg.

Aaron's eyes opened wide as he read the paper. "I can't believe you actually gave this to me. You father will lose the mine, you know. I hate to think of what he'll do to you if he learns you found this and didn't destroy it. I promise I won't tell him."

"You don't have to. I will. And you know what? It will feel good doing it...although I'm sure it will hurt afterwards. Most everything I've ever done, I did because he made me. Or because I thought it would please him. But I'm done with that. I don't want to be like him anymore. I don't want to lie and cheat, and hurt my own family. That's not honorable. A knight would never act that way."

"But he'll..."

"Don't worry about it. Worry about running the mine. The workers will be glad to have you back." Thomas laid his hand on Aaron's shoulder. "Merry Christmas."

"Merry Christmas to you, too."

"Does this mean we can have a fire?" Alice asked. The boys looked at her and grinned.

"You bet it does," Thomas said. He took the robe from Aaron and tore up part of a sleeve for tinder to catch the coal. Two strokes with the knife against the flint and the cloth was ablaze. The coal followed soon after, its intense heat forcing the cold air up and out of the chimney, opening the passage for the smoke as the logs finally began to burn in earnest. The wet wood sizzled and popped as the fire grew. Warmth crept back into the room an inch at a time. The children gathered around the fire and let its warm glow envelop them.

* * *

Kris opened his eyes and stood before the host of Elfs. "My friends," he said, "our mission is nearly complete. We delivered gifts to all the children in Oldenton, and in the process, we found proof of human virtue. Now only one thing remains."

"What's that?" Eldwin asked.

"We need to return home. Today, we shall rest and celebrate Christmas, a day with great significance for many human cultures. Now Elfs can share reason to celebrate! Today, we join in spirit with the people of Oldenton.

"And tomorrow...Tomorrow we rejoin our families in the Woodland Glen!"

A triumphant cheer arose, so loud that it actually filled the depths of the Great Northern Glen. It echoed through the crevice and rose into the air above like the hail of a trumpet, announcing to one and all that the Elfs were returning home.

CHAPTER 25
THE ELFS RETURN HOME

The next day the Elfs made six more sleigh cars and joined them together like a train. Four Elfs sat in each one, two in the front seat and two in the back.

"Are you sure you can pull us all?" Kris asked Donder.

Donder laughed. "Come on team, he doesn't get it yet. Let's show him again."

The reindeer took off, their hooves digging in the snow and then pawing at the air as they rose up, out of the crevice and off to the Great Glen.

The Elfs laughed and sang as they soared through the sky. As they moved south, the sun appeared on the horizon and trees dotted the landscape below. An eagle soared high in the sky. It spotted something on the ground and dove after its prey. The reindeer pulled faster and passed the eagle as if it were standing still.

The Great Glen of the Woodland Elfs appeared on the horizon. The trees waved in the breeze, welcoming the Elfs home.

The reindeer circled the Glen, searching for a place to land.

"This is different than one sleigh on a rooftop. There's no place to set down with this many cars," Donder called to Kris.

"What about that meadow? We'll fit there."

"We can't come straight down, we need room to slow down."

"Can you take us down on the river? It's frozen solid."

"That ice is way too thin to hold us all."

"How do you know?"

"I grew up in the Great Northern Glen. I'm pretty familiar with ice. You just have to trust me."

"Fair enough. Don't worry, I have an idea." Kris pulled the gold-trimmed red hanky from his pocket.

"You're crazy," Elaana said. "You can't use that!"

"Watch me," Kris said, and snapped the bag open. "Hold this." Elaana grabbed onto the trim. Kris reached in and pinched out a pocket. He stood on the seat facing the rear of the sleigh and jumped as high as he could. The sleigh cars went by underneath him in a blur as the pocket unfurled like a window shade. Kris landed on the back edge of the last car and teetered in the wind. His left foot slipped and he almost tumbled off the edge, but Eldwin grabbed his ankles and steadied him.

"Thanks," Kris said.

"Do I want to know what you're about to do?" Eldwin asked.

"Probably not."

Kris held the corner of the pocket in his teeth and he climbed over the back of the car and went hand-over-hand along the rails back to the first sleigh. He climbed aboard, disconnected the back cars, and let go. The pocket with six sleigh cars and two-dozen Elfs inside it zipped into the bag, which fluttered and flapped in the wind.

"Is that better?" Kris called to Donder.

"I think so, yes."

Kris turned to Elaana. Their eyes locked. "I have to tell you something."

"You can tell me anything."

Kris took several deep breaths while Elaana held hers. "My family is not in Oldenton."

Elaana stared at Kris dumbfounded.

"They are—" The sleigh bucked and Kris and Elaana almost flew from their seats.

"Hold on, it's windy and this may get rougher," Donder called. Kris and Elaana held on tight as the sleigh fought its way through the turbulent air. The reindeer landed in the small meadow. Kris climbed down with his sack, set it on the ground, and reached in and pulled out a pocket. He walked to the edge of the field and opened the pocket. Sleigh skids thumped on the ground. The pocket sailed over the Elfs' heads and zipped back into the sack.

"That was really weird," Eldwin said.

"Ho-ho-ho!" Kris laughed. "You did fine. Remember, we are not measured by the challenges we face in life, but rather by the steps we take to overcome them."

"And how shall we measure you, Kris Kringle?" Haelan's voice called from behind the trees. He entered the meadow with the other council members. "We did not expect to see you back so soon. I hope for your sake you have not broken the Rules in returning."

"I didn't. I have proof of human virtue. By virtue of Rule 3,095, subsection B, topic 19–F, we are all allowed to return..." Kris told the Council about Aaron and Alice, and the impact of their parents' death. He explained how Horace had double-crossed his nephew, and how he used Thomas as a bully.

Upon hearing that, Haelan said, "Kris, this is not helping. Do you realize you are providing proof of why humans *don't* have virtue?"

"Yes, I know it sounds that way, but I'm not finished..." Kris explained Thomas' drive to be a knight, his refusal to believe in Cinder Clouds, and the gift of coal.

"That's not enough. Thomas took the path of least resistance. He was abusing the situation to his own means. Typical human behavior," Haelan said.

Kris told Haelan about the will hidden in the chair leg. How Thomas found it, and had the perfect opportunity to destroy it, but he didn't. He explained to Haelan the probable results of that decision; Horace was not a gentle man. Thomas knew that, and still he made the sacrifice to do what was right.

Haelan said nothing. The Council deliberated on the evidence. Eventually, Haelan spoke.

"It is agreed. Kris Kringle, you have brought us proof of human virtue. You and the Elfs who accompanied you are welcome back in the Glen."

A cheer arose from all Elfs except one. Haelan looked over at Elaana, who was looking up at the clouds, counting them and saying what animal each one looked like.

"My daughter is trying very hard not to think of something right now. Why does she hide her thoughts from me?"

Elaana counted louder and faster.

"I sense it has to do with your family..."

Kristina walked into the meadow, her husband followed a step behind her.

"Tell us, Kris, how is your family?" Haelan asked. "You did find them, didn't you? After all, that was your goal."

Kris looked at his mother, who was twisting the belt of her robe into a tight knot. He smiled at her. Then a giggle turned into a chuckle which grew into a deep belly laugh.

"Ho-ho-ho! *Ho-ho-ho*! *HO-HO-HO*!"

Kris laughed so hard snot bubbles came out of his nose. After several failed attempts to speak, he finally blurted out, "My family is wonderful!"

Kris got his composure. "Let me explain. My attachment to the humans is something you will never understand. I *am* one of them. For so long I needed to be a part of their world...to be able to laugh and eat and sleep among them.

"Then I found Aaron and Alice. They were special. From the moment I first saw them I knew I would be involved in their lives in some way. And while we may be related, I realize now I can never live among humans. They are not my true family.

"Thomas asked me what I would get on Christmas. I told him 'nothing.' I was wrong, though. I did get something."

"We gave you that suit!" Eldwin said. Elaana elbowed him in the ribs.

"Ho-ho-ho! And it's a wonderful suit. But I received another gift."

"What?" Kristina asked.

Kris turned to her and took her hands in his. "I learned that I already have a family. A mother and father, a brother..." Kris walked to Elaana and got down on one knee.

"And with your father's permission, a wife."

Haelan put his hand on Kris' shoulder. "Stand up."

Kris stood.

"Kris Kringle, you are wrong."

Kris started to speak, but Haelan held up his hand. Kris looked at Elaana. An apology replaced the laughter in his eyes.

Haelan continued. "You said we will never understand your connection to the humans, but we do. We were afraid of what you could do, but we see now we don't need to be. You cast all humans in a new light for us. You are a special man, Kris Kringle. And you are an exceptional Elf. If I were to measure your worth and give you something I hold in equal value, I have only one thing in all the Glen to offer. But it is not mine alone to give."

Haelan embraced Elaana. "If you wish to offer this man your hand in marriage, you have my blessing."

Elaana smiled and held Kris' hands. "Kris Kringle, you are the most amazing person I have ever met. I would love to spend my life with you."

Haelan placed his hands on theirs. "Elfs of the Great Woodland Glen, Kris and Elaana stand before us today to make a pact, to dedicate their lives to each other, and to join their spirits as husband and wife. Does any Elf here object to this union?"

The silence was total; not plant nor animal nor any part of nature dared bring forth grievance against them.

"Let it be," Haelan said, and with those words they were married.

"Ho-ho-ho!" Kris scooped up Elaana and kissed her. She wrapped her arms around his neck and kissed him back. The noise was deafening; not plant nor animal nor any part of nature withheld its call of celebration.

CHAPTER 26
PREPARING FOR NEXT YEAR

The Elfs did not stay long before returning to the Great Northern Glen. This time, their numbers were tripled, Haelan himself among them. When they arrived they got to work immediately, expanding the toy factory and building new cabins.

Kris did not need to work hard to spread the word about next Christmas, when he would expand his operation to include all the children of the world. Alice, as always, was an exceptional gossip. With her help the children of Oldenton—and their parents—spoke of the wonderful gifts Cinder Clouds brought on Christmas Day.

People from town to village to city relayed the news up and down every street, road, and boulevard. Of course, as word spread, the accuracy of the accounts declined. In turn, some of the details were left out, and some of the details were exaggerated. The evergreen branch grew to be a tree, all stockings were an alternate gift receptacle (provided they were hung by the chimney with care), and any naughty child risked getting a lump of coal as a present.

Upon hearing the news of the mysterious man who would bring presents at Christmas, most people asked the same question: "*Who* did you say will bring the gifts?"

"Cinder Clouds," the children of Oldenton responded, sometimes faster than their lips could form the words. The degradation of enunciation led to an information obfuscation. That is to say, most people heard it wrong. As a result, the gift-giving man of mystery began to inherit many alternative names. Among them:

- **Cinder Clowns** *(there was supposedly an insane posse of them, and their specialty was juggling fire)*
- **Center Plows** *(a helpful farmer)*
- **Sinner Klaus** *(a German of very ill-repute, and not readily embraced by parents)*
- **Thinner Clothes** *(perpetuated by a child with a lisp, and not readily embraced by kids who wanted toys and not clothes for Christmas)*
- **Sander Crowns** *(someone who made fine wooden hats)*
- **Sinterklaas** *(and many other translations of St. Nicholas, leading to a long-lasting identity crisis)*

One name, however, stuck better than the rest, and it is the name Kris Kringle is known by to this very day:

Santa Claus.

CHAPTER 27
OUR TURN TO SHOW VIRTUE

Professor Hodgin flipped the last page, and stared down at the picture inside the back cover.

"What is it?" Jason asked.

"A map," his father said, squinting as he bent close over the picture. "But not just any map. It's a map to the Great Northern Glen. Look at these markings and tell me what you see."

Professor Nara scrutinized the drawing. "It's not Japanese, like the rest of the book. Juan, what do you see?"

"It's not Spanish, that's for sure," Juan said.

Jason looked at the symbols that surrounded the map and drew one of them on a piece of paper. "Just to be sure we're all seeing the same thing here," he said, holding up the paper, "is this what you see?"

His father, Professor Nara, and Juan all nodded. "I think it's Elfish writing. They didn't use their magic ink on the map, probably to help protect the Glen," Jason said.

"I bet you're right," his father said.

"You know what this means, don't you?" Jason asked. They looked at him with expressionless faces.

"It means we can't keep the book!" Jason said.

"What are you talking about?" his father asked.

"Dad, that's a map to the Great Northern Glen. The Elfs have stayed hidden for hundreds of years. If we let this book get out, they'll be discovered for sure. We can't be responsible for that. It's our turn to show human virtue."

"And how do you propose we do that? Bury the book back out in the snow for someone else to find? The next person to dig it up may not be as honorable as you are, Jason. We can protect the book."

"No we can't. It's too risky. Don't worry, this is all part of my master plan. We have to return it to its rightful owner."

"You mean give it to Santa? That's great, we'll just walk it on over there. Anyone read Elfish so we can make sense of these directions?"

"We don't have to find the Great Northern Glen. Kris Kringle will find us."

"Oh, I get it," Juan said. "You're going to set a trap, and use the book as bait. A Santa Trap. Do you plan to cage him? No...He'll probably just escape. If he can get up a chimney, he can get out of a cage. Oh! I know, use a glue trap like with mice..."

"No, Juan. Nothing like that. We don't have to do anything special. Just leave it to me," Jason said. "You just have to trust me with the book."

"You're taking the book, eh?" his father asked. "And where do you plan to take it?"

"Home."

"For how long?"

"Until Christmas. Dad, all we have to do it leave it under the tree on Christmas Eve! Santa comes to our house every year. Why try to find him when all we have to do is wait for him to come to us?"

"Professor Hodgin, your son is a genius." Professor Nara tousled Jason's hair.

"I knew it was a good idea to bring you up here. All who agree with Jason's plan say 'aye,'" Professor Hodgin said.

Everyone said aye.

"It's unanimous. Jason will protect the book until Christmas. And you all understand that you may never speak of this—to anyone, mothers, brothers, nephews, cousins, college roommates—until Christmas Day. Once Kris Kringle has his book back, it won't matter anymore."

"That's because nobody will believe us," Rebecca said.

"So be it," Professor Hodgin said. "I don't need someone else to believe me to know what is true. We know it. That's all that matters."

"Professor?" Juan asked.

"Yes?"

"I hate to be the one to melt the ice caps, but it's been a week since we first found this book. Considering we're not going to get rich off *Cinder Clouds*, shouldn't we get back to our research? We have two weeks' worth of work to do in the next six days..."

Professor Hodgin nodded in agreement. He closed the cover of the book and handed it to Jason. "You're in charge of this now."

"I know," Jason said. "The secret is safe with me."

CHAPTER 28
A CHRISTMAS GIFT

The team did finish their work in time. They worked round the clock to do it, but the continual sunlight made that relatively easy. When it was time to go home, Professor Hodgin locked the book in a special safe that would protect it from fire and water.

There was a door to the attic in the back of Jason's bedroom closet. His dad put the safe in the attic, to make sure Justin would not find it. It would also be safe from Jason's mom up there. Jason wanted to tell them both, but he knew they wouldn't be able to keep the secret. It was hard enough for him and his dad, and he went to bed every night hoping that the rest of the research team had kept their promises, too.

***

When Christmas Eve finally did arrive, Jason climbed into the attic and got the book out of the safe. He wrapped the book like a present and put a label on it:

To: Cinder Clouds
From: Jason

He set it under the tree, way in the back. Later, after he went to sleep, his father moved it to the fireplace, next to the milk and cookies.

And in the morning, the book was gone.

ACKNOWLEDGMENTS

Writing a book is a lonely process, but there are people along the way who bring wisdom, companionship, and the much-needed dose of reality every once and a while. For me, those people include my wife Angie and my sons Max and Vic; my beta readers—Laurel Montgomery Spatz (I owe you!), Sue Quinn, Joshua McCune, Scott G.F. Bailey, Jen and Hannah Sargent, Donne Hole, and my dad and Diane; Tracy McKenzie and her third-grade class, who believed I was a real writer before I believed it myself; Steve Sargent, Angela Moore, Melissa Abramowitz and the staff at Freedom Trail Elementary; Nathan Bransford for the advice and encouragement you give to so many writers, and for being such an excellent example of human virtue; the mods and lab rats at The Literary Lab for discussions that helped me grow as a writer and storyteller; the writers who participate in The Public Query Slushpile—never give up; and everyone else I forgot to mention.

ABOUT THE AUTHOR

Rick Daley lives in Lewis Center, Ohio with his wife and two sons, and a neurotic schnauzer named Leo. When he's not writing, he can be found playing his guitar or bass. He enjoys cooking, running, and yoga. He doesn't like writing about himself in the third-person and will stop now.

Read Rick's blog:
http://mydaleyrant.blogspot.com

Follow Rick on Twitter:
@rjdaley101071

Please read this.

It is

THE MOST IMPORTANT PAGE

of this book.

I'm glad that got your attention. First of all, thank you for reading my story. I really hope you liked it. Writing it was challenging, and it took a long time.

If you did like it, please tell a friend about it. Or enter a review on Amazon.com or another online retailers' site. Or buy a copy for everyone you know. Or have ever met. Whatever suits you.

This is a self-published book, and every voice counts!

www.CinderClouds.com

Made in the USA
Charleston, SC
16 July 2011